The Draconic Pipeline

The Dreamwalker, Volume 1

Matthew Summers

*To Bobbi
Hope you like it!*

Published by Matthew T. Summers, 2019.

Matthew Summers

Dedication

It's been a long road, but here we are. Wow. Just wanted to say thanks to Donna and my family, for always being there for me through this process... for my mom, who initially showed me the love of writing in the first place... to Jana, who's helped my writing evolve through the years... and to the folks at the Herscher Project and my friends from the web comic world, who have helped shaped my writing in so many ways over the years.

And a big thank you to Fiona Jayde for her fantastic cover to the novel!

PROLOGUE

"Watch out!"

The warning came almost too late. I heard the thundering "whoom-whoom" of the centidragon's feet as she skittered toward me, intent upon her dinner and heedless of the foolish biped standing before her. Instinct took over, and I dove to the side as the creature zoomed past and straight into her cage, her eight legs neatly missing me by only inches. The beast took little note of nearly trampling me, and the horse-sized creature instead greedily dove headfirst into her meal.

I pulled myself to my feet with a grin as the centidragon's younglings yipped in greeting at their momma. I took two steps toward her and placed a hand against her flank, still amazed at how soft the scales of the brownish-green creature actually were. "Silly beast. One of these days, she's going to flatten me."

From behind the stable wall Iri chuckled and shook her head, sending dust flying out of her blonde curls. I doubted I would ever get tired of that image. "She'd be awful sad if that happened, Mark. She adores you."

"I helped bring her into this world and helped keep her kits alive while they were still in their shells; of course she adores me." I smiled at Iri before I looked to where the first of the three suns had already crested the peaks of the mountains. "Going to be another hot one today."

"They always are." Iri whistled to get the attention of another set of centidragons. "I'll bring those two in." With practiced ease, the young woman hopped over the low stable wall and flashed me a brilliant smile. "Wouldn't want you to risk getting trampled twice in a day."

"Alright." I watched her walk away through the grass, and was struck again by both by how lucky I was, and at how odd this situation truly was. After all, I could still remember turning a wrench in those damnable Pipes. Lord, it seemed like so very long ago...

CHAPTER ONE – MARK SMITH

It was raining that day, the very first day I traveled from my world to the one that would become my home. It was nearly always raining there, a dusky, filthy sweat of a rain that did little to clear the mud and grime out of the daily life that I knew. On the few days that it wasn't raining, the bitter cold would turn the airborne moisture into something resembling a cross between a pathetic attempt at snow and a smattering of dust mites.

Living in the Undercity was not healthy by any definition, but we had little choice in the matter. We were Pipe Workers for the Corporation, and it was the Corporation that dictated where everyone in the Undercity lived. This was the absolute closest you could reside to the Pipes and survive, so this was where the Workers lived.

As was my normal routine, I waited with the rest of the crew members near the edge of the bus line, all of us cogs in a machine. The others would always stay just a bit further away from me than from other Workers. I had never quite fit in, and I'd always wondered why. All Workers were required to be about average height, yet I was taller. I had the same pallor to my skin and darkness to my hair as the others, but while most Workers were muscular, I was lithe and sinewy.

And they absolutely hated the way I talked. Claimed I was talking 'above' them, somehow. Said I was different. Like I could help the way I talked... I grimaced as the water from above dripped down, splattering into a watery demise against the poor fools that were forced to wait for the dilapidated bus that, once again, was running well behind schedule.

The boss was going to be furious. Again.

Near me, I heard an intake of breath as Joe Frazier, my neighbor, came to the same conclusion I'd just arrived at. I shook my head. "Might as well just get ready to get screamed at, Joe."

"I can't... can't take it again, Smith." Joe was shivering. He was always shivering. He'd told me before he had some condition, but to be blunt, I never paid much attention to what he, or what any of the other Workers, really said. Few of us paid any attention to what the others said to anyone else either; that was not what we did. I was there to do a job. We were all there to do a job, nothing more, and fraternization was frowned upon to the point we really weren't even supposed to talk to each other outside of work.

But how realistic was that, honestly? I'd been swinging the same wrench for six years next to Joe. We rode the same bus every morning and every night. Eventually, we'd learned each other's names. It was unrealistic of the Corporation to think we could go our lives without some basic human interaction.

I smiled, a half-hearted attempt at reassurance for Joe. "Sure you can, Joe. It's just the job, remember? You go, you swing your wrench, tighten the bolts, and then you go home."

"And then what?" Joe had an odd look in his eyes, a look I'd not seen there before. "What about tomorrow?"

"Well, tomorrow, we do it again, I suppose."

"And the next day and the next day and the next day and the next day..." Joe's voice trailed off into babble as he looked up into the rain. "It never changes, Mark."

I blinked. Joe had never called me by my first name, it had always been Smith. A few of the other workers around us began to take note of the way Joe was acting and edged away from us. Though uncommon, it wasn't unheard of for a worker to snap and go on a rampage; no one wanted to be nearby if that happened. "Now, Joe, there's nothing wrong with..."

"There's everything wrong with that, Mark," he interrupted me. "When was the last time you saw the sky?"

"The sky?"

"Yes, the sky." Joe swiveled and grabbed the front of my uniform, pulling my face close to his as he continued to talk. "The big sky above us, where the life-giving air that we breathe comes from. It's where this damnable rain falls from, and where the light is born. The sky, Mark. When did you last see it?"

"Er..." I was not comfortable being so close to Joe. I'd never paid much attention, but up close, the man was very unpleasant looking. Working in the Pipes as long as he had had left a pockmark of ruin across his face, etched permanently across his brow and down each cheek in rivulets of lines and creases. Hair poked out of random intervals from these folds of skin near his jaw line, thin and unpleasant. His teeth were long gone, replaced by the Corporation's dentists with the industry standard chompers that were pallid yellow. "I... I don't know if I've ever seen it?"

"You..." Aghast, Joe mercifully released me. "You can't be serious. You've never seen the sky?"

"I can't say as I have, no." I dusted myself off, thankful to have some distance between Joe and myself again. "I mean, yeah, I know what it is, but I haven't seen it. None of us have, you know?"

"You poor, poor fool." A sneer etched its way across Joe's face. His voice rose as he turned to the other workers on the platform. He threw his arms wide and shouted, "Have any of you morons seen the sky?"

Everyone simply stared back at him in a mixture of hatred, fear, and confusion. After a long moment, Joe started to laugh... a coughing, barking laugh that sounded like it was coming from deep within his psyche, ripping free from any bonds of sanity he had been clinging to until that point. It was not a kind laugh, and it threw his body around like a ragdoll, making his head loll left and right as he mocked us over and over.

Mercifully, at this point, the bus careened around the corner at a high rate of speed. Joe's eyes lit up as the bus approached. "You might not have seen the sky, Mark, but I have... It's beautiful. It's a bold blue with clouds that roll lazily across it, like they have nothing better to do, because they don't... because they're clouds, what else would they have to do...?"

"That's crazy talk, Joe." I didn't like the way Joe was looking at the approaching bus. "But..."

"Not crazy, Smith." Joe turned and his eyes met mine. To my surprise, his eyes were wet with tears. I couldn't remember the last time I'd seen anyone cry. "Not crazy... And now? Now it's just time I go."

"Go?"

"Yes. Go." Joe nodded at me, once, then turned back to face the bus. "I miss the sky, Mark. And I know I'm never going to see it ever again. I can't... I can't do this anymore."

"But Joe..."

"Goodbye."

I almost wanted to reach out to Joe, to grab his arm, to stop him from what he was about to do. But, why? What good would it do? The other Workers and I watched impassively as Joe stepped into the path of the oncoming bus and waited.

It took only a moment. The bus was automatic; no human sat at its controls, nor would they have given it a second thought anyway. With a thud and a sickening crunch, Joe disappeared underneath the metallic behemoth as it pulled up to our stop. The screech of complaining brakes filled the air as it ground to a halt, and the doors slammed open to let out the returning workers from their shift.

They filed past us, ignorant of the drama that had just unfolded, aware only of the fact they needed to go home and get some rest before their next shift started. As the last worker filed out, the green light above the door changed to blue, and it was our turn to board. As one, the assembled Workers and I took a step forward and filed into the bus, unheeding of the fact that the bus was sitting on Joe's corpse.

Once on board the bus, I settled against a smeared, ashen window and peered out as the bus doors slammed shut and pulled away from the stop. I tried to see behind us, but couldn't make out any details through the grime.

Joe's death was as inconsequential as his life. But as the bus continued on, his last words wormed their way into my psyche. Unwanted, unwilling, but there they were, burrowing into their new home. No matter how I tried to distance myself from them or change what I was thinking about, those words returned.

I caught my gaze drifting upward, and I forcibly yanked it back down to the floor where it belonged. Daydreaming was a fool's errand. If you didn't focus on your work, you would die; everyone knew that. It was drilled into you from the very first day you came to work.

So why did I still wonder what a cloud really looked like, and how could it possibly roll lazily? What did that even mean? I didn't know. I didn't even begin to know how to find out.

But still. How could it?

CHAPTER TWO – THE PIPES

No one spoke as the bus finally arrived at the docking station and pulled into its designated slot. No one dared. Inconsequential talk was for non-work hours, and even then was frowned upon. I could tell from a quick glance around that Joe's death was already long-forgotten, filed away in the repository of "things that just don't matter" in the lives of the men around me. Why I still dwelled upon it, I did not know.

The doors opened with a familiar groan of metal against metal, and we stepped forward as one, the acrid stench of the Pipes slamming into our senses immediately. There was a tinge within the familiar metallic burn; one of the pipes had been leaking, and a team was already at work fixing it. That tinge would be the composite materials they needed to repair the leak, and all hands would be needed immediately to help repair any and all leaks within the Pipes.

And we, of course, were late. Very, very late. The Boss was standing before us as we disembarked, his thin frame and disheveled hair a sharp contrast to the sheer hatred that seethed from his eyes as he surveyed us, one by one. Before he could scream at us, however, there were protocols to follow, protocols even he dared not disobey.

His eyes counted the workers assembled before us, six, twelve, fourteen, nineteen. Nineteen vacantly-staring lifeforms in vacuum-sealed trousers and a non-descript sealed vest. He paused when he reached me, the last man standing on his platform. The anger in his eyes mixed with a bit of confusion as he pointed at me. "You! Worker! Where is the thin one, the nervous one?"

Woodenly, I responded, "Dead, Boss."

"Dead?" he responded with disbelief. "He can't be dead. Do you know how much paperwork is involved if he is? How difficult it is to get a replacement worker? How's he dead? How, Worker, did he die?"

To not answer a direct question would put me in the same category as poor old Joe. I replied, "Stepped in front of the bus."

"Bloody hell." The Boss's voice rose as he started down his tirade. "Stepped in front of the bloody bus? Was he mad?"

Since the last question was again directed at me, I replied, "I think so, Boss."

"You think so?" The Boss frowned, deeply. His voice took on a dangerous edge as he said, "Workers don't think, they just do. Who told you to think? You're not being paid to think."

I knew I was traveling into very delicate territory. One word from the Boss, and I'd be into deprogramming for a month, and wouldn't even remember my name once I finished. "No, Boss, I'm not. But he asked me if I'd ever seen the sky, or a cloud. Then he laughed and stepped in front of the bus."

The Boss's eyes narrowed with suspicion, but he nodded slowly after a long minute. "Yeah, even a fool could see he was mad from that question, I suppose." He tapped his chin for a moment, studying me, before he turned to the man beside me. "You. Worker. Did you see this happen?"

The man beside me nodded slowly and replied in a deep baritone, "Yes, Boss."

"Did everything happen exactly how this Worker says it happened?"

"Yes, Boss. Sky. Stepping in front of the bus. All of it."

The Boss relaxed visibly. "Very well. I believe you." He motioned to the hub of activity behind him. "I'll get with the Corporation today and see about getting his replacement soon enough, I suppose. More blasted paperwork..." He shook his head and sighed deeply before he raised his voice again and snarled, "Now get your asses to work! We've got a ton of shit going on right now, and if you slugs don't get going, I'm going to dock each and every one of you a half day's meal paste!"

"Yes Sir!" Our voices chorused as one, and we sprinted to our toolboxes that were arrayed in a circle around a large metal platform. A few of us cast each other furtive glances full of relief. Joe's death might have seemed inconsequential, but it had managed to distract the Boss long enough to let him forget about the fact that we were nearly an hour and a half late.

I grabbed a large wrench and a small fusion blowtorch out of my toolbox before I strapped on my tool belt. Next out of the box came the safety harness, the full helmet, and two large, thickly-padded gloves that were the trademark of a Pipes worker.

I heard a clank of metal above my head, and I grimaced. Of course they'd start with me. Time was running short, and I didn't even have my safety harness on yet. I struggled to pull the straps over my head as the large metal claw began to descend to the Worker platform. I only just got the straps connected and latched when the metal claw hooked the harness's large metal hook and yanked me mercilessly off of my feet. It was only by the grace of God - whatever gods still paid attention to the ants that lived on this ball of mud anyway - that I managed to keep hold of my wrench, but I did.

While I dangled in the air like a macabre puppet, I pulled the rest of my equipment onto my body. Thankfully, by being first, I still had plenty of time to get ready; there were eighteen more Workers to pick up and move to the Work site, so I'd be ready long before we moved off of the platform. The metal claw paused only slightly when it reached the section of the platform where Joe's toolbox was; the news of Joe's death obviously hadn't reached the claw's programmers, and the claw took two attempts to grab at a metal hook that simply wasn't there. Finally, the overrides kicked in, and the claw moved onto the next Worker.

Once all the Workers were clustered around the rings of the claw, it pulled us into the air and we started our trip into the depths of the Pipes. The heat of molten lava blasted me in the face the moment we crested the edge above the platform, but the seal of my helmet against my pressurized vest protected my lungs from being vaporized from the inside out by the noxious gases and steam. As we dangled above the lava beds below, thoughts of Joe and his death drifted away and my focus returned to my work.

Ahead of us, the massive Pipes that came from the City far above were carved into the very bedrock. Each Pipe led to a different subsection, and I knew each and every single one of them by heart, even though there were easily a thousand of them in this section alone. Today's problem Pipe was a sewage drain pipe from City Level 42, Subsection Z19.

As we approached the Pipe, I saw the problem immediately. The strain of the sheer volume coming through the pipes had ruptured one of the seams, and the cracks had spread nearly two-thirds of the length of one section of pipe. Already, Workers were feverishly pouring over the damaged section of pipe, dangling from their safety harnesses while raw sewage poured out of the crack like a fountain.

In our helmets, the Boss's voice crackled into life. "Alrighty, boys, you're going to get down and dirty today. Good thing none of you slobs take baths anyway!" His laugher was harsh, grating, and truthful. "We're on the lower end of the Pipe, and I want to see our production up by 125% to account for the loss of one of my Workers. Since none of you losers even tried to stop him, I'm holding each and every one of you accountable for his death."

I grimaced. Getting to that kind of productivity level was impossible with a full team; with the loss of Joe, it was a literal pipe dream. But we had no choice.

The Boss continued, "We will have his replacement as soon as possible. Until he arrives, your production levels better stay up, or you will have me to answer to. Is everyone clear on this?"

As one, our voices rang, "Yes, Boss!"

"Good. Now stop standing around, hurry up and get moving! The paperwork's already killing me today."

I grimaced as the claw ground to a halt, slamming me into the Worker next to me unceremoniously. There was the screech of metal, and then the claw descended toward the pipe. Closer and closer we drifted, until the claw paused at exactly ten feet above the pipe's surface. With a hum of hydraulics, each Worker's individual section of the claw extended outwards, out and out and out, until each of us was a full twenty-five feet apart from the other.

Our work space now assigned, the claw jumped once and lowered again until our feet touched the pipe. Instantly, our boots clamped down to the metal, and as sewage poured over us, we began to work. Air that was only marginally better smelling than the outside environment piped into our helmets, keeping us alive even when the sewage poured out of the pipe and covered us completely. It was back-breaking work, it was thankless work, and it was fantastically filthy work.

But we were Workers. This was what we did, and this was how we did it. There was no other way to support those that lived in the upper echelons of the City above; without this, they would drown in their own sewage. They would have no power for their City. They would not have anything to go about their daily lives comfortably. So it was up to us, the Workers for the Corporation, to ensure that their lives were never once interrupted by something as simple as a burst sewage pipe.

Even if the pipe was large enough to fit a dozen buses inside.

It took fourteen hours before our team fully repaired the damage done to our section of the pipe. Fourteen hours of welding metal with only the gloves, helmet, and our basic clothing to protect ourselves from the steam of vaporized sewage, molten metal, and sparks that flew off of the fusion blowtorch from time to time. Occasionally, a swell of sewage rumbled from above, and if you weren't quick enough to move away from the crack, the spray would coat you from head to toe.

But finally, the crack was sealed, and the pipe's integrity returned to Corporation standards. Our job was complete for the day, and it was time to go home. The claw deposited us back on our platform by our respective toolboxes, and back into their places went our tools. After our gear was safely stowed, we moved to stand, rank and file, to board the bus once again. The Boss was nowhere to be found, which was no small relief; getting yelled at the end of the day was a tradition that none of us minded missing.

Once on board the bus, I found my thoughts divided. On the one side, I felt a slight bit of pity for those that would have to take this blasted bus after us; the smell coming off of us was downright vile. Granted, it was part of the job... but still, I felt a small twinge of guilt.

My thoughts also meandered back to Joe. He'd been so willing to throw his life away, just because he'd never see the sky again. I'd never seen the sky before, so I couldn't begin to imagine what it was about it that would possibly inspire a broken shell of a man to throw his life away like that, just because he'd never get to see it again.

All because of the sky. It made no sense. At least then, it didn't.

I hesitated once I'd stepped off of the bus, though none of the other Workers with me did so. They bustled past me on their way to their hovels, eager to start their sleep cycles and feed on the meager sustenance the Corporation shipped down to us for our pay. The Workers that were waiting to board the bus also paid me little attention, and pushed past me once the green light signaled the bus was clear for their entry.

I waited for the bus to depart before I examined the dry stretch of road where Joe had perished sixteen hours prior. The cleanup crews had been around, unfortunately, only a small darkened smear marked where Joe's body had possibly been. It was too hard to tell if that smear was simple grease, a leak from somewhere up above in the regular City, or what remained of Joe's lifeblood. He'd been effectively erased from the world, like all of us were the moment we died.

I shook my head and sighed. There was no point in fighting it. This was the life of a Worker. And if I didn't get back to my hovel soon, my scraps would be automatically cleaned up and I would miss my meal for the day, which would make tomorrow a very long day indeed. Luckily, I was one of the few Workers that had a hovel within a hundred meters of the bus stop, so it didn't take me long to return home.

The door to my home opened automatically as I approached, and I stepped into the small room with chagrin. The moment I entered, a small door to my left slid open and a robotic voice intoned, "Deposit."

Automatically, I replied, "A minute, please." I stripped out of my clothing as fast as I could, dropping the rags into the space behind the door as I did so. The moment the last article of clothing hit the ground inside, the voice intoned, "Received," and the door slammed shut.

Another door slid open to my right, this one wide enough for me to step through. The same metallic voice said, "Enter." I did so without comment, and the door slid shut behind me. I was immediately blasted from all directions with a powerful, cold blast of water that lasted for precisely seven seconds. Then the warmth of the detox waves kicked in, and I sighed with relief as the next ten seconds were actually comfortable.

A quick blast of air to shake off the excess water and the door slid back open. I stepped out into the small room and took my clothes from the open receptacle. They were warm, at least, and only smelled slightly of sewage; it would take another time or two in the cleaning process before that smell was completely gone.

After dressing, I took three steps forward to where my meal waited. The grey mush looked just as appetizing today as it had every day for the prior twenty-eight years, but it beat having an empty stomach. After choking down the food, I took another step to my left and sat down on the bed, having crossed the entirety of my home.

Such was the life of a Worker. I collapsed on the bed, the exhaustion of the day heavy on my bones. Joe's words disappeared as sleep gripped me in an iron grip of blissful slumber. My last conscious thought was that, perhaps, I could dream about what it might be like to see the sky.

Just once. Just... once...

CHAPTER THREE – TO SLEEP, PERCHANCE TO DREAM

My sleep that night was deeper than normal. I do not often dream; few Workers do, for what would we dream about? Our daily lives? No, my sleep normally was just a solid state of blissful unconsciousness, until I eventually got cold. Once I got cold enough, I would awaken once to adjust my sleeping position, and then fall back asleep until the designated sirens went off to wake the Workers. It was a routine I'd done for what of my life I could remember.

However, my sleep that night was different. Unlike before, I did not shiver in my sleep; I actually felt quite comfortable and warm, a warmth unlike anything I'd ever felt other than during those few seconds when I was purified from the day's contaminants. It was oddly comforting and relaxing. And long before it was my designated time to wake, I felt a pulling, a desire to open my eyes, a need to awaken that I'd never felt before. Try though I might, the urge was inexorable, unyielding, and annoyingly stubborn in its persistence.

I began to wake, my consciousness begrudgingly returning from the pleasantness that was oblivion. My first thought was it was unusually bright in my house. That meant something was either shorting out, or there was a fire somewhere. The Corporation kept light levels in the shacks set to fixed levels in order to keep the majority of usable energy flowing to the upper levels of the City. The Workers did not rate, nor need, much light; this much had to be a problem.

My eyes opened, and I looked up... up... up... and beyond. Something was different. Instead of the grey roof of my home and the single Corporation light fixture I'd seen for at least the last decade or so, there was literally nothing at all over my head. Far, far above my head stretched an expanse of incredibly blue material, intensely blue...

Was... Was that the sky?

In shock, I sat up, trembling. A quick glance around me confirmed my suspicions. The home was gone. I was no longer lying on a slab beneath my familiar sheet; instead, I was lying on the ground, atop some thin-bladed plants that were oddly soft. I reached out to touch them, but I could not bring myself to pull them out of the earth. Instead, I let the softness of their blades rest in my hands for a moment before I jerked my hand back as if I'd been stung.

My gaze returned to the blueness above me, and I tried to think of what I knew about the sky from what little schooling was given to a Worker. The sky existed above the City, I knew that. It was blue, at least if it wasn't polluted or raining or covered in clouds. And clouds were white, grey, or black. And there would be a single sun.

The sun. That would be the source of the light that was so blasted blinding. I turned my head, quickly pinpointing the brightness of the twin orbs that blazed in the heavens. It took me nearly a full minute to realize that there were two suns staring down at me, and a third just peeking over the edge of the horizon, way off in the distance. Oddly enough, it was at this point that I started to relax.

After all, I was now certain this had to be a dream. The Earth only had one sun. That fact had been established long ago, long before the formulation of the Corporation, long before the construction of the planet-wide City, and long before anyone alive could even remember. So that meant that, surely, I was still asleep in my hovel, and having the first dream I could remember having in at least a decade.

I slowly pulled myself to my feet, stretching as I did so. For a dream, it was remarkably warm and extremely vivid; perhaps there had been something in the sewage that had affected me. Yes, that was it, I reassured myself as I turned my gaze to my surroundings. Surely there had been something inside the sewage that was causing this dream, because I certainly had never had a dream this colorful in my entire life.

I was standing in what appeared to be a field, if the fog that clouded my memory was feeding me the correct information. Surrounding me were more of the bladed plants, all no higher than my shin. Far, far off into the distance, I made out what appeared to be much larger plants with solid stalks, and bunches of appendages on the top that held some form of fluffy material outward toward the three suns. If my memory wasn't lying to me, they were called "trees." I must have seen one at some point in my past, because otherwise how my dream knew to paint one was beyond me – though by the same token, given that I had no idea what they SHOULD look like, perhaps my subconscious was merely making something up?

My thoughts were making my head hurt, so enough with that. I shook my head to clear it and continued looking around me with interest. The trees ringed the field I was standing in before melding into the horizon where the third sun was rising. From the other direction, away from the triple suns, a small plume of smoke rose over the trees. It was jarring against the blue of the sky, and I studied it for a long moment.

Finally, I spoke, my voice sounding alien and unwelcome in this pristine paradise. "Well, I suppose there's nothing to do but explore, is there?"

The plants at my feet did not respond. Whatever had been in the sewage, though powerful, wasn't fully hallucinogenic. I was free to enjoy myself without the need to report to the Clinic in the morning for a full cleansing. With nothing else to do, I began to walk toward the smoke.

I do not know how long I walked, though by the time I reached the first of the trees, the third sun had risen fully from behind the mountains and joined its brethren in the skies, and the day had gone from pleasantly warm to downright hot. The shade brought by the trees was welcome, and I sat against one for a bit of relief. The stalk of the tree was surprisingly rigid, almost like steel, though it had a softer exterior crust I was able to pick off with my fingers to inspect. With only a bit of pressure, the crust crumbled under my fingers, and though it still held some of the rigidity of the stalk, there was softness to it I didn't understand.

It did not, however, taste very good.

After I'd cooled down enough, I continued my trek toward the smoke. Without any way to judge distance in this dream though, soon enough the familiar touch of fatigue began to set into my legs. It was obvious I would soon have to find a spot to rest.

The realization brought me to a complete halt, and I stood there amongst the trees, befuddled. How long had I been walking, anyway? This was easily the longest continuous dream I'd ever had, though who knew how time was judged in dreams? I glanced up at the sky, but the triple suns were heavily obscured by the plant life overhead. The trees in this section were grown together, and their upper appendages were intertwined with each other's, forming an effective barrier against the heat of the day and preventing me from seeing the position of the suns from where I stood.

There was a break in their appendages farther away from me, but I was simply too exhausted to walk any more. I slumped down against one of the stalks and put my head down into my hands, still trying to process what was going on.

How could I be tired? Wasn't this simply a dream? Could you get tired in a dream? I didn't know the answers. I only knew what the feelings that my legs and body were telling me, and I'd never walked so much in my entire life. Years of working the Pipes had conditioned me for hard labor, but that was hard labor in one specific spot; you rarely, if ever, moved more than a few dozen feet away from your workspace.

It would often be fatal to do so, after all. Falling off of a pipe was rare, though not unheard of. And the molten lava that was below the majority of pipes was very unforgiving of any Worker that had his safety harness fail.

Granted, it probably beat being run over by a rickety old bus. At least burning to death was quick.

I yawned and tried to get comfortable against the stalk of the tree, with varying degrees of success, until finally I gave up and decided to lie on the ground with my head against a small protrusion that jutted up from the very base of the tree.

That seemed to do the trick, and I found the light of my dream slowly dimming as I fell back into a deep sleep.

CHAPTER FOUR – BACK TO REALITY

I was out of my bed and moving before the first siren had a chance to begin blaring. With a clang, my plate of food arrived, and the same grey glop as always squirted onto it from the designated food dispenser; breakfast was served. I rubbed my eyes and inhaled the food before the realization sank in that I was home.

I looked up at the ceiling, a part of my subconscious still stuck in last night's dream and fully expecting to see the expanse of blue sky stretching above me. Instead, thankfully, the bleak grey ceiling and single light stared remorsefully back, uncaring at my disappointment. The trees were gone, the bladed plants at my feet were gone, the fresh air had vanished, and everything was as it had been.

It had been nothing but a dream.

I sighed deeply and shook my head. "Dreams and wishes do not a Pipe repair. Focus on your work, or fall into Despair." The mantra I'd learned in school was fresh in my mind, I repeated it over and over as I finished my breakfast and walked out of my hovel toward the bus stop.

A new man was already waiting at the bus stop, a tall, thin man who stood at attention as he waited for his fellow Workers to arrive. He nodded in my general direction as I approached, and I grunted by way of greeting. No other words or motion passed between us; he was not Joe. I did not know him or his name, and though that might come in time, right now, he was just another Worker, like I was.

And we were waiting on the bus with the rest of the Workers. The bus that was late. Again.

As the rain started to fall, I found my thoughts returning to the dream I'd had the night prior. It seemed so vivid, so real... I could still feel the crust of the tree stalk crumble between my fingers, the firmness of the tree underneath my hands, and the heat from those three suns warming my body. But it was nothing more than a dream.

I was startled out of my reverie as the Workers on the platform pushed forward, shoving me into the waiting bus. I had not noticed it arrive, nor had I noticed when the Workers from the shift before ours departed. I shook my head to clear my thoughts; getting lost in thought and daydreams was a sure-fire way to die when working the Pipes.

I grimaced as the bus pulled away from the stop. My legs were killing me. Unconsciously, I rubbed my calf muscles, massaging them as best as I could in the cramped confines of the bus. They were in knots, which was unusual. I could understand my back or arms hurting, but my legs? I moved very little yesterday.

Wait. My legs hurt. Like, my legs really, really hurt. But that didn't make sense, very little of a Worker's job required leg movements. But yet they hurt. My legs and feet hurt like I'd spent hours walking on an uneven surface.

Like I'd spent time walking... across many lengths of short-bladed plants to reach trees?

My eyes grew wide, and I started to shake as I looked at my hands. No. No, there was no sign of any residue from the tree stalk's crust on my hands. It had been a dream. The pain had to be a side effect from sleeping so deeply last night. The Corporation would have known immediately if I'd left my hovel, and I'd have already been arrested and detained to await my trial. But I was on the bus, and nothing was different, nothing had changed.

It was a dream. It had to have been a dream.

I spent the rest of the ride down to the Pipes feverously trying to ignore the dull pain in my legs and feet. If any of the other Workers took notice of my plight, they paid it no heed; we were not there to have concern for each other, we were there to do our job and return home, nothing more. But for once, I feared returning home, for returning home would mean returning to sleep, and then what if I dreamed again?

No. I steeled myself and tried to shake off the lingering doubt. No. No, I would not go down that path. I was a Worker, nothing more. Dreams were for children, and for those that lived in the City. I had a job to do. As the bus came to a stop in the depths of the Pipes, the dream was finally forgotten and I was ready for the day.

The Boss was oddly pleasant, especially considering we were, as usual, late, thanks to the bus. He barely looked up from his workstation as we assembled, and he dismissed us to our workstations with only a quick "Dismissed." It'd been years since any of us had seen him this pleasant.

Getting the new Worker must have been considerably easier than he'd thought.

Today's pipe repair was another massive section of the same sewage pipe we'd worked on the day before. As always, the large claw descended and pulled us into the air, and we set to work. Thankfully, no sewage flowed through the damaged sections of piping today; previous Workers had managed to divert the flow to prevent any further pressure within this pipe, allowing for a complete repair.

This allowed the fusion blowtorches to work at their optimal levels. Yesterday they performed adequately while covered in gallons of raw sewage, now they performed to manufacturer guidelines. Sparks and molten metal flew in a cascade of lethal fireworks from each Worker as we feverishly worked to seal off the fissure in the pipe. Below us, the molten lava pool greedily accepted our debris without care; dropping a wrench or fusion blowtorch was not something any Worker wanted to consider.

Finally, our shift was over, and we waited in rank and file for the bus to arrive to return us to our hovels. The Boss still hadn't said a single word to us; this was the happiest we'd ever seen the man, and it gave me a sense of satisfaction to know that, at least in a small way, the work I'd done today had to have contributed to whatever it was that was making him happy.

Tomorrow, I'd redouble my efforts personally. The longer we kept the Boss from shouting at us, the more likely it was that we might actually get something in our food ration other than grey mush. I couldn't remember the last time I'd eaten anything with another color to it.

Pleased with the idea of eating better than I had in years, I boarded the bus to return home with the rest of the Workers, and for the remainder of the ride I tried to imagine what red mush would taste like. Or blue. Or maybe even green mush. The possibilities were simply endless.

As we disembarked from the bus, the new guy caught my eye and nodded. "See you tomorrow, I suppose?"

"Hmm? Oh. Uh. Yeah, suppose so."

He jerked a thumb at my hovel. "That yours?"

"Yeah." I nodded.

"How do we get bigger?"

"Bigger?" I blinked in surprise. "You don't. Why would you need bigger?"

He shrugged. "The Worker that lived in mine before was too short. I stick out. I can't sleep."

"You'll get used to it." I'd already talked to him more than anyone other than Joe. And I had tolerated Joe. This Worker, I didn't like. He didn't know his place. "Goodbye."

"Bye."

I watched him walk away for a long moment, before I shrugged and walked to my home. So the new Worker was strange. He couldn't be any stranger than Joe, after all, and Joe threw himself under a bus. I wondered idly how long it would be before this Worker threw himself under a bus.

As before, the door to my left slid open, and I automatically stripped and dropped my clothing into it before I stepped into the cleansing zone. By the time that was done, my food was waiting for me; grey sludge again, so however happy the Boss might have been, it hadn't been happy enough to affect our food rations. Once the night routine was complete, I sat back on my sleeping pad and started to close my eyes.

Then I remembered the dream, and my eyes flew open. I sat up, though fatigue was already pulling at my frame, trying to drag me to slumber. No matter how much my body might want it, I needed to resist sleep for a minute. I did not want to chance having that dream again. Workers were not allowed medicine except under extreme conditions, but perhaps a bit more liquid would help keep the demons away.

I swung my feet back off of the sleeping pad and stood. A voice intoned, "Request?"

I responded with, "Water."

There was a pause, followed by, "Granted. ETA sixty seconds."

I waited, and in exactly sixty seconds, a small vial of brackish water was delivered in my food delivery area. I popped the lid off and drained the water with a grimace before I placed the vial back onto the designated slot. As it was sucked back to the Corporation for reuse, I sat back down on my sleeping area and closed my eyes.

I felt my stomach revolting against the excess water I'd put in it, and I smiled. There would be no deep sleep tonight. Satisfied, I allowed myself to fall asleep, and the darkness claimed me again.

CHAPTER FIVE – DREAMS, REDUX

I heard a slight sound, a sound I couldn't remember hearing before, a screeching that was not metallic or man-made in origin, just at the edge my hearing. I tried to ignore it as sleep held me in a firm grip, but the sound was persistent, drilling into my subconscious like a knife. It cut through the walls I placed before it like I would cut through the Pipes during a repair, deftly cleaving all obstacles I tried to place before it. Finally, I gave up and woke, determined to find and silence the source of the noise.

It was incredibly bright this morning. It took me a full minute to realize I was lying on the soft, thinly-bladed plants, and my head was resting against a hard piece of something that jutted from the ground, and that hard piece of something bore a striking resemblance to the stalk of the tree I was lying underneath.

I bolted upright, my pulse racing in my ears as the world swam before me. It couldn't be... but there, all around me were the trees from my dream. I'd returned to the exact place that I'd left. But how was that possible?

I looked down, and on the ground was a small piece of the tree's outer shell, discarded with a small indention from my teeth. I'd carried the piece I'd tried to eat as I walked yesterday, enjoying the overall feel of the small piece in my hand. I remembered finally releasing it as I began to fall asleep, here in the dream. I shook even harder at that point, and forced myself to remain standing only by sheer force of will.

Why was this dream torturing me so? I heard the sound that had woken me again, this time a bit louder and off to my right. I turned, but could not see the source of the sound. With nothing better to do,

I did what my dream bid of me, and followed after the sound. It didn't take too much walking before the sound intensified; whatever it was, it wasn't all that far from where I'd slumbered.

Finally, I stumbled into a small clearing in the trees, and the source of the sound was revealed. A small animal of some sort was standing on what looked to be the remains of a tree, garbling away making the noise I'd been following. As I entered the clearing, the creature stopped and peered at me warily.

I, too, stopped and studied it. The creature was barely bigger than my hand, with an oddly cylindrical body that was covered in a colorful blue pattern. Beady eyes peered from the top of its head, and some form of protection covered where its mouth would be. Thin, skeletal legs popped obscenely out of the base of the creature, and claws jutted out from those legs to grip the tree remains with ease. It looked rather frightening, though thankfully it was small enough that I doubted it could do much harm if it decided to attack me.

I took a step toward it, and to my complete and utter surprise it took flight. It opened limbs that were hidden against its body and, with a quick hop, simply took into the air with a grace and ease that I envied. It flew up to safety in one of the nearby trees and continued to peer down at me, watching carefully.

I do not know how long I stood there, agape in wonder, until I regained my senses and shook myself back to reality. I muttered, "This is really quite some dream," and walked over to the remains of the tree the creature had been standing on. The tree appeared to have been dead for quite some time, I guessed. I didn't really have a way to tell, but the weather had not been kind to the exposed interior. I wondered idly what killed it. I was running my hands down the smoothness of the tree's exposed center when it hit me.

The lines of this dead tree were far too perfect. I recognized a skilled hand when I saw it, and something or someone had cut this tree. Cut it down, and done so with a precision of a Worker, perhaps even a

Tradesman from the middle circles of the City! Intrigued, I examined the husk closer, and sure enough, there were little markings along the exterior of the dead tree. Something had cut it, and obviously that had ultimately led to its death.

I looked around. None of the other trees had been killed like this. Why this one? And by what, or by whom? What was special about this particular tree? And where did the rest of its body go?

The blue creature decided I wasn't a threat, and began to warble again. I glanced up at it, but it was no longer my concern, so long as it didn't decide to attack. I thought back to the smoke I'd seen yesterday. Smoke meant fire, and fire needed some sort of fuel to burn. Were trees flammable? Perhaps that had been the source of smoke I'd seen.

If that was the case, then perhaps there were other people in my dream? I wasn't sure I wanted to know, but as I didn't have any other options, I cast my eyes to the sky to see if I could spot the smoke I'd seen yesterday.

Up in the brilliant blue of the sky, the three suns burned merrily away. They were partially obscured, however, by an assorted variety of massive puffs of white smoke that seemed to come from everywhere. It was impossible to tell where this sheer volume of smoke could possibly be coming from.

Something Joe had said to me suddenly echoed in the back of my brain. I paled as I whispered, "You might not have seen the sky, Smith, but I have... it's beautiful. It's a bold blue with clouds that roll lazily across it, like they have nothing better to do, because they don't... because they're clouds, what else would they have to do?" My legs gave out at that point, and shakily I sat down on the corpse of the tree while I stared straight into the sky.

After a few moments, I could tell the smoke was, indeed, moving very slowly across the sky. It was moving exactly as Joe had described it. So that wasn't smoke... It was... "Clouds. Those are clouds. By the Corporation..." My pulse pounded in my ears again, and I brought my gaze down to my hands, which were shaking. I clasped them together in a wry attempt to force them to stop as I stood back up.

That was a mistake. My legs were not nearly recovered yet from the shock I'd just been through, and I tumbled to the ground with a grunt. I tried to brace myself as I fell, and I yelped as a sliver of the dead tree worked its way deep into my hand as a reward for my efforts. I grimaced and dug at the sliver, but it was too deep. Though it did not bleed, there was no way I could get it out of my hand without access to any sort of tool.

"Foolish Worker." I shook my head and carefully got back to my feet, testing my legs before standing fully this time. Though my hand hurt, it wasn't all that bad; only a bit of a twinge where the sliver actually was, and as long as I didn't put too much pressure on it, I barely even noticed it.

I turned my gaze back to the sky, but the problem I'd had before was still apparent today; even in the clearing, there was only so much of the sky I could see, and I could not tell where the smoke I'd seen before had come from. The only thing to do at this point was choose a direction and go. So I did the only logical thing I could think of... I used the mountains in the distance as a guide, put them to my back, and walked away from them, deeper into the trees.

I walked for hours. The trees grew thicker and thicker together, until it seemed that they were going to eventually grow on top of each other. They were also joined by smaller plants, plants that grew no higher than my waist. These plants were very full in appearance, though upon closer inspection I determined it to be a false show; they were merely smaller designs of the tree tops, attached to very thin tendrils of tree stalk.

As I walked, I noticed more of the tree carcasses that had been deliberately killed, just like the one I'd found earlier. And, also like before, only the shorter remains of the trees were left behind; where the rest of it went to, I had no idea. I also started to see considerably more of the flying creatures with the strange cylindrical bodies. They avoided me with little effort, and I began to relax when it became obvious they didn't mean me any harm.

Eventually, the skies grew dark and my legs burned from the exertion of the day. I sighed and found a suitable tree stalk to prop myself up against as I felt the iron grip of sleep approaching once again. I wondered idly if I'd return to this exact spot tomorrow night when I slept. I carved a few random x-marks in the damp ground to show where I'd been.

Above me, I heard a few warbles of noise, and I glanced up into the tree and met the eyes of one of the creatures that flew. It ignored me, beyond to keep a wary eye on the strange creature below it, as it continue to call out its racket into the heavens. I smiled up at it and said, "You keep doing that, I'm not going to hurt you."

It didn't respond, of course. I doubted that it could. I chuckled again at the absurdity of my dreams and closed my eyes, ready to return to another productive day of work. Gradually, the warbling dimmed as darkness enveloped me, and I slipped away into a deep sleep.

CHAPTER SIX – THE NEW GUY

As usual, I was up and moving almost the moment the siren claxon began. The morning routine was underway; eat and out the door to wait for the bus to be late. Nothing was different today, either, same grey interior as every other day, same non-descript hovel, same everything.

So why did I expect something different? "Foolish Worker," I muttered to myself as I gulped my morning meal and headed out of my home so I wouldn't miss the bus to the next worksite. Of course, the bus would likely be late again, but occasionally the Corporation found it necessary to give the bus the repairs it needed, and it would run on time for a few months. Woe be the Worker that missed the bus because they'd gotten used to it coming late!

I was early, earlier than I normally was; my dream from last night still lingered in my memories. That wouldn't do... distractions were lethal. I shook my head, rubbing at a slight pain in my hand to try to chase my memories away. I heard the new Worker approaching, and though I tried to ignore him, he stood close to me.

The new guy sighed deeply and peered at me. "Sleep well?"

This again, with the talking. Fine. "As well as a Worker should."

"I suppose I did. Still too short of a sleeping mat. Can we request a larger mat?"

The absurdity of his question hit me like a wrench aside the head. I gaped at him in openmouthed horror until he finally cleared his throat and said, "Er... I suppose not." He shifted from one foot to the other before he continued, "You don't talk much."

"I'm a Worker. None of us do."

"Ah." He digested that for a minute, then said, "And Workers don't talk because?"

"Were you not trained?" I glared at him.

"Beyond a basic 'do this or you die'? No."

"No?" I didn't respond for a moment, stunned. I'd never heard of a Worker that wasn't trained. All of us were groomed for the job from about the time we turned six. It was an insanely dangerous job if you weren't trained. "Where did you come from?"

"I'm from the City."

"Oh. Oh..." Realization dawned on me, and I smirked. "A criminal."

"No!" The new guy shook his head so hard I wondered for a moment if he was trying to unscrew it. "No criminal! I just..."

I jerked a thumb toward the City above us. "You're not up there anymore, are you?"

"Well..."

"You did something the Corporation didn't like."

"Well..."

"And they punished you by making you a Worker."

"Not punished, exactly..."

"Yes or no?"

"Fine!" Exasperated, the new guy threw up his hands in disgust. "Yes, I wound up on the wrong side of the Corporation, and they sent me down here to punish me, but I'm no criminal, damn it all." He pointed a finger at my hovel. "Do you like living here?"

I blinked at the sudden change in the conversation. "Why would I not?"

"Oh please." He spit in distaste. "You eat grey sludge. You sleep on uncomfortable slats of metal, barely padded with cloth. You are power bathed to prevent infection, but there's no comfort, there's no sense of individuality, there's no humanity down here. You're a cog, my friend. You're less than human."

"I'm a Worker." I didn't quite understand most of what he was talking about, but I was beginning to understand how he ended up down here. Even in the City, the Corporation would not stand for talk like that among the people.

"No. You're a human being. You have a soul, you have a presence, you have a name, you are a living, breathing person. You're not just a tool, an insect inside a hive tending to the Queen."

"You're insane." I turned my back on him at this point. None of this was anything I needed or wanted to hear. Talk like that would lead to confrontation with the Corporation.

"You poor, deluded man." The pity in the man's voice grated on my spine, but I refused to turn around. "How many years have you been toiling away down here, hmm? How many years have you given to the Corporation, only to have them repay you with nothing in return?"

When no answer was forthcoming, he sighed. "Fine. You can't run away from me, you know. I'll be here every morning and every night."

I refused to answer, and after another period of silence, he shook his head and turned his back. The both of us waited for the rest of the Workers to arrive at the bus stop in silence. I continued to rub at my sore hand unconsciously, my annoyance for this new Worker growing.

How dare he come down here and speak like that. A Worker's place was serving the Corporation, everyone knew that. I resolved to avoid him as best as I could. Though he was right... every morning and every night, he would be able to confront me, though all I had to do was not listen. Not listening was easy, to a point. The last thing I wanted to do was wind up on the wrong side of the Corporation.

He may have fallen from grace and wound up down here, but from where I stood, the only thing further down than where I was standing was a wide expanse of molten lava. I grimaced as the pain in my palm increased under my rubbing. Damn this hand... this pain was going to be distracting today, I could tell.

But where did the pain come from? I couldn't remember injuring my hand yesterday while working on the Pipes, and certainly not while I was sleeping. So then what...? I looked at my hand and did a double take. Embedded near my ring finger was a small sliver of something unidentifiable, sunk deep in my hand. I could tell that it was in there quite deep, and I'd need my tools or something sharp to cut it out...

The realization of what it was hit me like a wrench against a steel pipe. My knees buckled, and it was only through sheer force of will I managed to keep to my feet. The nearby Workers glanced at me, but I steadied myself quickly enough that they went back to ignoring me.

It couldn't be.

It just... it couldn't be. I plunged my hands deep into my pockets and stared straight ahead, ignoring the twinges of pain as I waited faithfully with the other Workers for the bus to arrive.

It couldn't be. I numbly boarded the bus once it finally arrived, and the ride to the job site was a complete blur. I stared at my hand for the entire trip, the noises and low hum of the bus a distance second to the glaring irregularity staring back at me from deep within my hand. Robotically, I exited the bus with the others, and though the Boss was yelling I heard none of it.

It simply could not be. The claw descended and plucked me off of the platform and away we went. I did not know what Pipe section we were to work on; I simply went to work to repair what damage I could see, each slam of the hammer or twist of the wrench pulling a twinge of pain from the piece of whatever it was that was lodged within my hand.

Finally, the day was over, and it was time to go home. Before I knew it, I was disembarking and the new guy was saying something to me. I didn't notice what he was trying to say, as I ignored him entirely, shoving my way past him and making a beeline toward my hovel.

Once inside, the voice intoned, "Deposit," and I replied, "Wait."

The voice replied, "Waiting. Command?"

I held up my hand and said, "Inspect wound."

A red light bathed me from the ceiling, followed by a quick "ding."

"Inspection complete. Small foreign object detected in forehand. Analysis complete, common wooden compound. Simple removal process, insert hand in receptacle." A door to my right slid open.

I placed my hand inside the small door, and a bright red light burst from within. After a moment, the voice intoned, "Removal complete. Resume day?"

I looked at my hand as the door slid back shut. Sure enough, the sliver was gone. My voice was shaky as I replied, "Y... yes. Resume day."

The rest of the day was spent lost in thought. Common wooden compound. I knew of wood, at least in general, as a construction material used mainly in the upper reaches of the City. This deep into the Undercity, wood was simply not found; everything was dirt, rock, metal, or plastic. It couldn't have come from anything around me.

Perhaps the new worker had brought it from the City above? Perhaps, but then how would he have inserted it into my hand, without the Corporation sensors going off at his intrusion? No. No, the object in my hand had to have come from that tree in my dream. But the computer had said 'common wooden compound,' so did that mean that trees were made from wood?

All questions. No answers. As sleep approached, the only thing I was certain of was this... The dreams were getting more and more vivid, and if I'd carried over this speck of wood from my dream, what else could make the transition?

And what could it mean? As darkness overtook me, I still only found questions in my mind.

CHAPTER SEVEN – DISCOVERY

The rain was cold, and I shivered in my sleep. It was odd, to feel rain dripping on my slumbering body. My roof was supposed to keep the rain out, at least marginally; granted, it wasn't in anywhere close to what one could call "good shape," but I did try to maintain at least some form of watertight integrity to the roof when I could. The Corporation engineers came around once a year to inspect our homes, and we were required to help them patch any issues they found. But to have this much water striking my body bode ill of their and my skills; they weren't due back for quite some time, so I'd have to figure out how to replace the entire roof.

As the rain intensified, I grimaced and reached down to grab my thin blanket, hoping to protect myself against some of the rain. When I could not find the blanket, I stretched further down my body. Surely the blanket was gathered down by my feet somewhere...

A loud voice rumbled from beside me, "Well, it's about time you moved, human." The voice was intense, at a volume just a shade lower than excruciating and it was a deep baritone with a heavy growl within.

Years of waking up for the Corporation had conditioned me to spring awake, at the ready in a moment's notice. An unfamiliar voice from directly beside me was a better alarm than any I'd experienced to this point. Without hesitation I sprang to my feet, my eyes coming into focus as I gained my footing on the wet plant life I'd been sleeping on.

As I'd half-expected, I was back with the trees, in the very area I'd fallen asleep in the night prior, most likely against the very same tree. Unlike my prior dreams, however, the day today was not bright and sunny; the skies above were dreary and overcast, not much unlike the environment of my home, truth be told. Large droplets of water fell from somewhere above, splattering themselves against anything they encountered and generally soaking everything to the core.

It occurred to me that I'd never seen a real, full-on rain experience before, as most moisture that reached into the Undercity still had to filter down through the City above and brought the grime with it; this was a beautiful thing to behold. If I'd awoken on my own volition, I probably would have spent hours just watching it.

However, the one glaring difference between this dream and my other dreams was not the rainfall. No, this difference was much more obvious. Not twenty feet from me lay a massive creature that was regarding me calmly through the rain. The head of the creature alone was the size of the bus that I used every day. Its body was an ashen grey and covered in closely-fitting connected plates of some material I couldn't fathom. Large protrusions of the four-legged beast jutted out into spikes from each of its joints as well as from its large, toothy maw.

The beast was heavily muscled beneath the plates and, though it was massive in size, large, delicate wings were tucked against its back. Those wings extended down to its haunches and the thought that something of this size could fly boggled me. A long, serpentine tail trailed away into the trees beyond, hidden only partially by the underbrush.

No creature, living or dead that I was aware of had remotely resembled such a beast as this magnificent thing that was peering at me with an idle curiosity. I shook my head in bemusement. My dreams were getting stranger.

The creature's gaze never wavered as I stood. When it spoke again, I realized the deep baritone growl I'd heard before had come from it. "So you are alive."

"So it would seem." I looked up at the sky, letting the rain hit me in the face before I returned my gaze to the creature.

"You... are not concerned?" Genuine surprise registered in the creature's voice.

"Concerned about what?"

The creature raised its head to gaze at me with both of its eyes. "Concerned about me."

I wasn't entirely sure how I should answer that statement. "Should I be? I mean, obviously you've been there for some time. If you meant to kill me, you'd have done so already." I motioned to the ground. "How long was I lying there? You're massive; one step, or one bite, and you could have killed me, but you didn't. So I don't see why I should worry."

"Interesting." The creature chuckled, an odd-sounding laugh that came from somewhere toward the center of its chest. "I've never met a human that didn't run away in fear from the moment they saw me. It's a rather... unique experience."

"Fear? Workers of the Corporation have fear beaten out of them as young children. Fear can lead to hesitation, and hesitation can lead to death when you're working on a Pipe." I shook my head. "No, mindless compliancy is much more preferred of an emotion than fear."

"I'm afraid I don't quite follow you, human."

"That doesn't surprise me." I sighed, changing the subject. "This whole dream is a new experience for me." I motioned down the length of the creature. "So what, or who, are you, anyway?"

"Dream?"

"Yes, dream. This." I indicated the rain above. "This... rain. The plants, the... trees? All of this. This is all a dream. You, even. I don't understand how, but this is all a dream. It has to be."

"Well, that would at least explain a little about how you appeared next to me while I was resting." The beast blinked, slowly, as it watched me. "So tell me, human. What other aspects of this, 'dream', seem to make it so?"

"Everything. The three suns in the sky. The lack of sharp smells in the air..."

"Pardon my intrusion," The creature said, interrupting me, "but what do you mean by, 'sharp smells'?"

"It's hard to explain." I took a deep breath, savoring it. "But put simply. There's no stench of burning metal, there's no acrid chemical smell, and the air isn't stale, overused, rejected. It's simply... there. I've never smelled the like."

"Where, exactly, do you come from, human?" The creature peered at me again. "Nowhere in my travels have I smelled burning metal, unless I've directly caused it myself."

I sighed. "I come from the Undercity. At the behest of the Corporation, I live where they chose for me to live, so I live deep within the bowels of the world. I work on the Pipes so those above can have a good life."

The creature studied me for a long time without speaking. Finally it murmured, "From your reactions, you do not prefer this world. You want to go home, to your world of metal air."

"I... I don't know. I think I do. Yes. I do. I mean, why wouldn't I?" I sighed and sat back down against the tree as the rain continued to fall. "I don't understand what I'm seeing here. I can't even imagine how I'm dreaming these things – none of what I've seen here is like anything I've experienced in life. So I can't understand what exactly, my dreams are pulling from for inspiration. It's frustrating and distractingly dangerous for my job."

"Well..." The creature paused, carefully considering its next words. "What if this isn't a dream?"

"That would raise more questions than I'm comfortable addressing." I shook my head. "Would you mind a few questions of my own? I don't feel like talking about my home any further."

"Of course." The creature nodded, the movement rustling the trees overhead. "By all means, ask me anything you'd like. I'm having one of the most interesting conversations I've had in over a hundred years."

"A hundred years?" I stared at the creature with wide eyes. "Most people in the Undercity barely make it to their sixties, even with the Corporation's medicines. How old are you, exactly?"

"Oh, a few thousand years or so. I've only within the last few hundred years entered an age where I'm able to mate, so I've still got at least three to four thousand years left before I'm ready to fly over the oceans to the lands beyond." There was a seriousness in the creature's voice that left no question as to the truthfulness of the statement.

"A few thousand..." I shook my head in disbelief. "Um, alright, next question. What are you?"

"Well, that would be obvious to anyone from this world. But, as you said, this is all rather new to you." The creature fixed me with a strange stare. "I, my human friend, am what is known as a dragon."

CHAPTER EIGHT – DRACONIC DISCUSSIONS

"A dragon?" I shrugged. "If the word is supposed to carry some meaning to me, I'm afraid it does not."

"Of course not." The creature looked up into the sky, letting the rain drizzle down its face as it talked. "This is not your world. You know not of the mighty dragons, nor of how people fear us and try to kill us."

"Fear you?" I raised an eyebrow. "Kill?"

"Aye." The creature motioned toward its flank. "Take a closer look at the scales on my flanks, human."

"Er, alright." I wondered idly if I should be wary of this 'dragon' now, after what it had just told me. I reassured myself that, if it had wanted to hurt me, the creature would have done so long ago. I stood and picked my way through the underbrush until I could easily see the lower end of the creature's serpentine form. It took a few minutes; the creature was quite long. And once there I saw what it meant. "Ah, yes, I see some heavy scarring. Is that..."

"Indeed." The dragon sighed. "I was feeding, and did not pay attention. A group of humans got close enough to me to attack, and that was the end result. I wasn't able to fly for weeks until I healed."

"Ah, you can fly. I'd wondered that." I studied the scar tissue – the damage had been pretty severe from what I could see. "It looks like you got rather lucky; this looks pretty nasty."

"Indeed."

"Why would they attack you?" I reached a hand out, involuntarily, toward the long-healed wound. I stopped myself before my hand grazed the creature's form.

"Do you know much about magic, human?"

"Magic?" I looked back toward the dragon's head, meeting its gaze. "What is magic?"

"Hah! A deeper question than you probably realize!" Amused, the dragon blinked and looked up toward the sky. "But have you noticed some of the trees in this forest have been brought down, while most have not? And only certain trees?"

"I have seen some trees down, yes, but I didn't realize they were only certain trees."

"They are specific trees." The dragon looked back down to me again. "The humans use those trees for their magic, and they would use my scales, teeth and bones for their magic as well."

"Oh." That didn't quite make sense, but enough of it did. "And the humans that attacked you?" I figured I already knew the answer, but it had to be asked.

"I do not savor the taste of human flesh." An edge came to the creature's voice. "But for that one instance, I made an exception."

To attack a beast such as this, I could think of easier suicides. "They were fools then." I shook my head as I walked back to my tree to sit back down.

The creature watched me wordlessly until I'd returned to my sitting position. Finally, the dragon said, "Fools? Why?"

"Fools for attacking you. For attacking any, what'd you call yourself, a dragon? Fools for attacking dragons in general." I shook my head in disgust. "This, right here. You might be different from anything I've ever seen, but so what? You could have harmed me long before I ever woke up, but you waited patiently for me to wake instead. I've never understood violence of any sort; it just never made sense."

There was another long stretch of silence before the creature continued, "You are quite unlike any human I've ever encountered. And it is my pleasure to converse with you." The dragon considered something for a moment before it said, "I have a wonderful idea. This world, in all its glory, is not experienced well from the ground. Would you like to see this world as I see it?"

"How you see it?" I blankly looked at the dragon. "What do you mean?"

"From the air."

I swallowed nervously. "I'm not sure I'm very comfortable with that idea."

"Come." The dragon brought its head down to the forest floor. "Sit on my neck, just behind my head. You should have plenty there to hold onto; the scales won't harm you."

"Er." This seemed like a very bad idea. But still... when in dreams, it's best to do what the dream tells you to do, same as in life. "Alright."

I stood and walked back over to the dragon, studying the neck as I approached. Up close, it dawned on me just how massive this creature really was. It looked like the best avenue of approach up to its head would be to first step on what looked to be its shoulder, so I did that.

After a moment of scrabbling up the dragon's muscular neck, I seated myself in a small recess toward the back of the dragon's skull. I placed one hand around a small bony spike and another into the scales near where I was seated. As the dragon had indicated, the scales were thick but not sharp by any means; my grip was quite firm. "Alright. Now what?"

"Now hold on. And if I drop you, never fear, I shall catch you. I will apologize ahead of time, I fear if I have to catch you, I might wound you with my claws. So I'd prefer if you just held on, my friend."

Holding on sounded perfect. "I'm ready."

"Very well. Be mindful of my wings, they're about to unfold."

With the sound of ripping fabric, the creature's wings snapped open with a pop to either side of me. I felt the dragon tense below my legs. I gripped with both my hands and legs as the creature threw itself into the air.

The leap was an incredible show of strength; one single jump took us above the height of the trees in a mere moment. Once clear of the trees, the dragon's wings unfolded fully, catching the air and propelling us forward and up with a single downward thrust. The dragon's wings were easily five or six times the length of the creature's entire body. They must have been doubly and triply folded up against each other to have been so small against the creature, but it made sense that they were so large in order to support this gigantic creature in flight.

Then the reality of what I was doing hit me, and I was at once both terrified and exhilarated. It only took a few moments until I began to relax; this was much more enjoyable and considerably less jarring than being hoisted into the air from the Worker's platform, and no Worker was scared of heights, after all. As the wind whipped my eyes, I looked around in wonder while the trees grew smaller and smaller below us.

What I saw was astonishing. The trees stretched out to the horizon, broken here and there by tracts of what looked like some form of blue liquid; water, perhaps? The mountains I'd been keeping behind me actually stretched in every direction, encircling the trees in a massive, protective wall. Using them as a guide had been, at best, a futile gesture. I could see that now. I could not tell if anything lay behind the mountains, and there was no way I could ever walk far enough to find out; the distance was simply too vast.

I tried to speak, but found that between the rush of the wind and the beating of the dragon's wings, my voice was completely drowned out. With that option gone, I contented myself to simply enjoy the ride.

That's when I noticed it. Off to the left, in the vague direction that I had been walking, a large section of the trees had been removed and the ground cleared away. Beyond that section, structures had been erected in a fashion that was odd to me. Instead of stacking each building against the next for efficiency, there was space between the buildings. I could not discern what, exactly, the buildings were made of or what purpose they served; what mattered was that it was definitely a sign this place was inhabited by someone. Even at this height, I saw movement around the buildings.

The dragon, perhaps sensing where I was looking, angled its flight into a steeply-banked turn. As we approached the buildings directly, I saw it was more than just buildings. It was a small... town? Village? I couldn't remember the proper term; given that my home was an entire world comprised of a single city, such terms were tossed around and forgotten quickly. There were tell-tale signs of people living in this place: smoke rising from chimneys, primitive vehicles of some fashion scattered here and there, and other assorted items that, though I didn't know in particular what they were. They were obviously fashioned by human hands.

Around the edges of the village - I settled on village, it felt most appropriate – were some form of tall reedy plant that moved with the wind. The plants were, unlike the trees I'd passed through to this point, in oddly symmetrical rows, though how they came to be that way was beyond my grasp. As we drew near to the village, I could discern humanoid shapes as well as other, larger four-legged shapes milling about.

It was about that point when the inhabitants of the village noticed us. Granted, the dragon was neither small nor subtle; I imagined it would only take one or two of them looking up into the sky to spot us. The movement at the village increased dramatically, with shapes vanishing into buildings as word of their visitor spread. Soon, the village was deserted, at least from my viewpoint, and the dragon angled its flight into another turn, carrying us away from the village.

We flew for a time, away from the village and deep into the mountains. The weather broke and the combination of the air rushing past and the warming glow of the three suns quickly dried my sopping wet body. My idle thoughts as to where the dragon might be taking me were answered when we came to a rest in a wide rocky ledge underneath a large overhang.

The dragon landed on the ledge with a grace belying its great size and, after folding its wings back against its body again, bent its neck down to the ground and said, "You may dismount, my friend, this is safe ground."

I went to speak, and found that words, for the moment, were not forthcoming. So, in silence, I gingerly made my way off the dragon's head and clambered down to the ledge, careful to not get too close to the edge. After a moment, once upon solid ground, my voice finally returned, and I managed to squeak out, "That... That was quite a ride."

"Ah." There was a hint of pleasure in the dragon's voice. "I was afraid from your silence that you did not like flying. I see now this was not the case."

"That was... I don't... The words just aren't there. I don't know the words." I shook my head and walked to the edge of the ledge, my gaze taking in the vast forest and mountains below. "This world... this dream, if it even is a dream... it's absolutely beautiful. That's the word. Beautiful."

"Indeed it is." The dragon nodded. "And now you understand more as to why I wanted you to see it how I see it. There's only so much one can see from the ground level; sometimes one has to look at things from another perspective in order to fully understand life. Such is the way of things."

"That is not the thinking of the Corporation." I closed my eyes, basking in the warmth of the suns. It was considerably warmer here in the mountains, though not yet unpleasantly so. "It is their way of thinking, and that is the only way of thinking that is allowed. Any other way is criminal."

"I do not think I would like your world."

I couldn't believe the next words out of my mouth, even as I said them. "I... I'm not sure I like it much anymore, either."

CHAPTER NINE – MEETING THE FAMILY

The next hour or two – it was hard to mark the passing of time - was relatively peaceful. The dragon excused itself and disappeared into a large tunnel in the mountainside, leaving me alone with my thoughts. The longer the day went on, the warmer it got, so soon enough I had to pull myself away from the ledge and the view of the world and into the shade granted from the overhanging rocks above. The dragon had mentioned that it would grow warm as the three suns climbed into the sky, but as they descended it would get downright chilly; for now, it was well on the balmy side, and I was thankful for the relief afforded to me by the shade.

Eventually, the sounds of heavy claws on stone announced my host's return, and I nodded in greeting as the dragon appeared back out of the blackness of the tunnel. "Welcome back."

"Thank you, human." The dragon settled down comfortably against the rock face away from me with its tail draped over the ledge and into the abyss below. It appeared to be a favorite lounging position. "My apologies for being gone so long, my friend, but I had to check on my children."

"Your... children?" I blinked. "Ah, so does that mean your... um..." I grasped for the words, not finding them. I shook my head. "I can't quite make what I want to say come out."

"Then allow me." The dragon turned and studied me for a moment. "Are you asking about my children, or information about my mate?"

Oh, so it was the same word the dragon had mentioned earlier that I was grasping for. Feeling silly, I said, "Ah! Mate! That's the word. Yes. I wanted to know about your mate."

"The father of my children will never meet them unless it's by accident somewhere far down the future." The dragon gazed off into the distance. "Dragons do not form family units like humans do. When dragons mate, the male courts the female for a few decades. Then, once mating is complete, the male flies home, wherever that might be, leaving the female to rear the children once they hatch."

Hatch? "Ah. Well, that did at least answer one vague question I had in my head," I sighed ruefully.

"Then answer a more-specific question of my own, my friend." The dragon stared at me with curiosity. "This world of yours... As horrific as it sounds from what little you've told me, do they at least call you by a name, or are you little more than an insect to them? You do have a name, do you not?"

"A name?" I blinked. It was a legitimate question, I suppose. I'd not thought to bring it up. After all, back home, it usually took years of standing at the same bus stop before one Worker even bothered to find out another Worker's name, though my current annoying new neighbor was throwing that standard to the wind.

I realized I'd not answered her question and said, "My apologies, I was lost in my thoughts there. My name is Mark, Mark Smith."

"Well met, Mark." The dragon closed her eyes and dipped her head slightly. "You may call me Cerridwen."

"Ker... dwon?"

"Close," There was amusement in her voice as she repeated her name again, "but not so harsh on the first part, and lighter on the last part. And it's got three sections, not two. So Keh-rhid-when. Say each part slow first, then together."

"Ken."

"Keh."

"Keh," I corrected myself, even as she corrected me, "Keh-rid-when?"

"Very close." The dragon nodded. "Now say it as a complete word."

"Cerridwen?"

"Exactly."

"That will take some time to say correctly, I'm afraid." I smiled rue-fully and glanced down the tunnel she had exited from. "So how many children do you have?"

"Three dozen and two."

"That... wow." I suddenly found myself full of questions; Curiosity was a vice to be suppressed in most areas of my life, but now, without the specter of the Corporation hanging over my shoulders, it was like a weight was slowly being lifted from my body. "So how do they... I mean, what do they eat... how much...?"

I paused, holding my hand up to stop myself. "Wait, that's too many questions and to be honest, I don't know where all that came from."

There was a touch of mirth to Cerridwen's voice as she said, "Watching those emotions play out on your face was well worth it, hu-man. You really have been bottled up inside for a very long time, haven't you?"

"I'm not sure what you mean." I took a deep breath, and then con-tinued, "However, one question at a time. First. Thirty-eight children. How?"

"How is easy. I'll show you." Cerridwen considered something for a moment. "However, I do not know all that much about humans. How well can you see in the dark?"

"That depends." I shrugged. "Some of the Pipes are not in very well-lit sections of the Undercity. As long as there's some lighting, I can usu-ally function pretty well. In total darkness, however, I'm blind."

"Then let me show you something else first." Cerridwen turned her head away from me and continued, "The interior of my home is completely dark, but I can improvise. Not knowing what a dragon is, you would not know this, but I can provide you a source of light."

"You can?"

"Yes. Like so." She inhaled, and with a low growl, a blast of flame erupted out of her mouth and into the skies. The flame, initially reaching well past her mouth, was quickly pulled back until the fire only just barely licked out from between her teeth. Cerridwen turned her head at this stage and looked pointedly at me, allowing the flame to dissipate as she said, "I can maintain a low flame like that for some time to allow you light, though I will not be able to speak while doing so."

"Ah. Understandably so." I was beginning to understand the 'how' humans would fear dragons, if not necessarily the 'why,' at least. "If I can't see unless you're doing that, should I just try to follow behind you to avoid getting stepped on?"

Cerridwen shook her head. "No. Climb back on my neck, and I'll be careful as I walk to not dislodge you."

It sounded reasonable enough. "Alright." I stood up and walked over to the dragon. It only took a moment to scramble my way back up her neck; now that I knew what to look for and where to grab, it was an easy matter to retrace my steps.

"All seated?" Cerridwen kept her head still as I got myself situated.

"Ready to go."

"Good. Now, once we're in the tunnel that leads to my home, we can talk freely, but it will be too dark for you to see. When we're inside my nest, I will provide some light for you; let me know when you wish me to speak again, and I'll stop my flame so we can speak."

"Sounds good." I felt a strange flutter in my stomach as the dragon turned and started to walk into the tunnel. Was it nervousness?

...Fear?

Regardless, I was committed to the act, and as the light dimmed behind me, I had no other choice but to hold on as the darkness of the tunnel encompassed us both.

CHAPTER TEN – INTO THE BOWELS OF THE EARTH

I do not know exactly how long it had been since I was last in darkness as total and absolute as it was in that tunnel. Most of our worksites were at least fairly well-lit. There had been a few, of course, where sections of the Pipe remained buried underneath earth or other construction materials, so I had been in some dark, cramped crevices in my time.

But this darkness was absolute. This darkness laughed in the face of the three suns outside of its domain, and dared even a single ray of light to attempt to encroach upon its borders.

I could tell as the dragon continued walking, that the pathway sloped down somewhat. I felt the air getting cooler, and the pressure inside my ears registered the slight drop in altitude. But, for the life of me, if we made any turns, or if there were any side passages, or anything of that nature; I'd never have known it.

I cleared my throat. Below me, Cerridwen paused for a moment. "Yes, my friend?"

"How large is this tunnel?"

"Large enough for me to walk comfortably, but not so large as to allow me to spread my wings. It's smaller nearest to the entrance, but down here it opens up nicely." There was an amused tone in her voice. "Why?"

"I'm trying to work out how this tunnel came to be here. Is this something you dug, or...?"

"Oh no. These mountains are very active. At some point, this tunnel was completely filled with molten rock which wore away. That was long ago, though; it has been dormant for some time, and I do not expect it to erupt anytime soon, if ever again."

"Ah, so we're in a lava tube."

"A what?"

"A lava tube." I considered for a moment how to explain to Cerridwen what I knew about them. "Basically, when the lava is flowing slowly instead of erupting, the exterior of the magma flow will be cooler than the interior. If it's allowed to get cool enough, it'll return to regular rock, insulating the remaining magma and allowing the pipe to stretch further and further away from the eruption source."

"You are strangely educated for someone who, by your own admission, is barely even allowed to think for himself."

That stung. "Well, the Corporation provided us some basic instruction as youths, and then once we were assigned to our route in life, our education was geared specifically toward our set job roles. Lava tubes make for good pathways for new pipe. The Pipes reach down to layers of magma throughout the world, and it's a Worker's job to keep them operational. So most of us are familiar with magma."

"I see." Cerridwen didn't sound convinced, but she let it drop.

"Speaking of seeing... how, exactly, can you tell where we're going?"

"You humans have limited senses." Cerridwen's claws clicked against the stone as she walked. "When there is light, I see in likely the same fashion as you do, with color and definition. When light is not available, however, all dragons can still see; I cannot explain it how it works, I'm afraid, but there is no color or contrast created by colors when I am in total darkness like we are right now."

"So you can see, right now, with the same clarity as you did outside, just without color?"

"Indeed."

"I can think of a few times that would have been handy." I said as I lapsed back into silence.

I do not know how long Cerridwen walked, nor how deep into the mountain we went. If I'd thought time was impossible to track before, it was a fool's dream to attempt to do so now. Finally, after what seemed like an eternity, the dragon came to a stop.

There was a tinge of something in her voice this time when she spoke, though I did not know what it was. "We are here, human... Mark. Can you dismount without sight?"

"Um... I don't know." It hadn't occurred to me until her question that I wouldn't really want to mount or dismount her head while flame was coming out of her mouth. "I suppose there's no better time to find out."

"A moment." I felt the dragon lower her head until contact was made with the ground. "There. Even if you fall, it won't be far."

"My thanks." Carefully, I climbed down the dragon's head. It was odd, to maneuver down such a massive creature completely by touch, but it could not be helped. When my foot made contact with the ground, I only stumbled slightly before righting myself. "Alright. I am down."

"Well done." There was movement in the darkness, and when Cerridwen spoke again, it came from above me. "My flame isn't so bright to need you to look away and I will aim the initial burst safely to the side. Are you ready?"

I didn't really honestly know the answer to that question, but it seemed like it warranted a response, so I replied tentatively, "Yes?"

The dragon chuckled at my response, then took a deep breath. A wave of heat burst over me as flame erupted from Cerridwen's mouth, blasting away from me and toward the ceiling of what I saw was a large, expansive cavern. After a tic, she drew back the fire until, as before, flame barely licked out from her mouth, and she turned to look at me.

The visual of this dragon peering down at me with flame illuminating her face from within was unnerving, but that was quickly washed away as my gaze fixated on the cavern features.

I'd been in a few caves in the past, usually while running new pipe. Caverns were deemed dangerous usually, and left alone. Once the pipe was in place the caverns were typically filled and closed up with various leftover building materials. Concrete, debris, and the like would shore it up to prevent potential collapse. After all, rocks falling onto a line was never a good thing.

But those caverns had all had one thing in common – they were all a dirty, dusty, and grey, mirroring the dullness of my world. There was rarely any color, and if there were, it came from minerals within the surrounding rocks and was usually very muted.

This cavern was not muted. It was massive, easily large enough to hold Cerridwen a few times over. The walls I saw were streaked with a brilliant bluish-gold streak, from some ore I had never seen before. Depending on how the light shone, the walls appeared at once gold, then the next moment a deep blue.

Moisture dripped from far above, stalactites forming stalagmites over the centuries one layer at a time. From somewhere in the darkness, I heard the sounds of moving water, an underground stream, perhaps, and possibly the reason Cerridwen resided here. Access to fresh water this deep underground would be quite a boon.

It was beautiful, a word I barely remembered how to use. But an apt description it was.

Near us was a large pile of oval stones, each about the size of a man and speckled with orange and grey colorations. The ground around the pile was well scratched and worn; obviously Cerridwen spent considerable time here.

When I finally found my voice, it sounded alien and wrong in the wondrous surroundings I stood in. "It... it's amazing, Cerridwen. I've never seen anything like this. What gives the walls this coloration, if I may?"

She rumbled in response, an amused grunt, the flames in her maw dancing with the small release of breath. I shook my head. "Right. Can't talk. Got it."

I walked over to the nearest wall, bypassing the mound of stones to run my hand across the wall. It felt... warm and just slightly wet, yet when I removed my hand my skin was completely dry. "Whatever this ore is, it's not one I'm familiar with."

My attention returned to the rest of the cavern, my gaze coming to rest on the mound of oval stones. "But I don't understand. Where are the children you spoke of, Cerridwen?"

The dragon rumbled, once, and with a final flash of light the flames extinguished. She cleared her throat with a growl, then replied, "You are standing next to them, human Mark."

"I am?" In the total darkness, I, of course, couldn't see again, but I'm positive I wouldn't have missed thirty-eight creatures directly beside me. "I do not..."

"Did you see the clutch of eggs?"

"Eggs?" I tried to recall what I'd seen around me. Then I tried to recall what an egg was. "Um..."

"Do they not have eggs on your world?"

"The term is vaguely familiar," I lied.

Cerridwen sighed, an ominous effect given I couldn't see anything at all around me. "My apologies, my friend. Your world really is unlike my own. Did you see the orange-tinted objects near you, by chance?"

"The oval stones about as big as I am? Yes."

"Those are my children. They are eggs."

I made no attempt to hide the surprise in my voice. "Oh! Um..." I froze where I stood, afraid to move. "I'm not going to hurt them if I bump into them, am I?"

"They are encased in shell as strong as stone. I'd be rather impressed if you could do anything to them. Mind you," Cerridwen continued, and a warning tone came to her voice, "I would not be very happy if you were to try to harm them."

"Why would I do that?" It was exceedingly difficult to remain perfectly still. Without any sort of visual identifier around me, it was almost impossible to tell if I was moving or standing still.

There was a pause before Cerridwen continued, "My apologies, Mark. When it comes to my children, it's difficult not to be defensive. But I know you won't hurt them, or I wouldn't have brought you here." She paused, then continued, "This is not your world, and you are not like the humans here."

"However, it would be for the best if we return to the entrance of my home." There was amusement in her voice again. "You look like you're trying your absolute hardest to not move even a muscle."

I sighed in relief. "I would like that very much, yes, thanks."

CHAPTER ELEVEN – RETURNING HOME

The return to the cave entrance was rather uneventful. A few times along the way back, Cerridwen would pause and illuminate things for me with her fire. A tunnel junction covered in a white metallic substance. Another cavern similar to her own off a side path, with more of the bluish-gold ore streaks through its walls. A deep pool of water with blind creatures swimming in it that Cerridwen called "fish."

Apparently, though difficult to catch, Cerridwen deemed these "fish" quite tasty. I abstained from having a taste, not ready yet to experience everything this world had to offer.

Finally, a dim light cut through the darkness ahead of me, and the opening of the tunnel came into view with each step. I sighed in relief once I could fully see Cerridwen's head and body below me. "A Worker is not afraid of the dark, but where your eggs were is considerably darker than what most Workers are exposed to."

Cerridwen sounded concerned. "I won't take you back to my nest if you're uncomfortable there, friend. I wouldn't want..."

I interrupted her. "No, that's alright. I enjoyed seeing where you live, and all of this is so new to me. Those... eggs, you called them? You said they are encased in stone? So then, if those are your children, how do they... I mean... How..."

I grappled for a moment with my vocabulary, irritated at my inability to vocalize what I was trying to ask. Finally I shook my head and said, "Well, anyway, those are your children? So then, when do they leave the rock egg?"

Cerridwen replied, "Right now, if I were to break an egg, the interior would look nothing like a young dragon. Inside those eggs, magic is happening. There is a liquid in there, nothing more, for the time being. But in a few years, the liquid will change into a very young dragon, and eventually my children will scratch their way out from the inside. At that point, they will look like very small copies of myself."

"Ah." That made absolutely no sense, so I changed the subject. "So this will be your home for a few years then?"

"More than a few years. Barring something untoward, I'll live here until I feel the need to fly over the oceans to the lands beyond. So a few thousand of your years. I'll likely raise a few clutches of eggs in the very spot you were standing."

"Interesting." Fatigue was beginning to wear on me. How long had I been awake now? Awake, asleep... I still wasn't quite sure what was happening, exactly, I was while here. Was it a dream, or as Cerridwen seemed to think, another world entirely? If that was the case, then when was I sleeping?

"Mark?"

"Hmm?" I hadn't realized I'd fallen silent for some time while deep in thought, but we were now back at the entrance to her tunnel. Two of the three suns were well on their way over the horizon, and the third sun had started its journey down as well. As Cerridwen had promised, with the suns going down the temperature was considerably cooler than it had been, though it was still warmer than it was inside the tunnel. "Oh, we're here."

"Indeed." Cerridwen lowered her head to allow me to climb down, and then fixed me with a gaze. "You seemed to be thinking of something, and I did not see a reason to interrupt."

"I was." I paused, unsure even if I should ask the question. But hell, I'd gone this far. "Is... is this a dream?"

"From your point of view, I do not know."

"Well that's helpful."

Cerridwen stepped carefully as she moved away from me to lounge on the stone outcropping where we'd first arrived. She let her tail hang over the edge into the abyss below as she got comfortable. Finally, she turned back in my direction and she said, "Well, it's the truth."

A thin plume of smoke rolled out of her mouth, and she let it creep its way to the sky before she continued, "From your point of view, I'm not sure how or what I would even be able to believe is the truth. Your world sounds so very, very different from mine, this world must seem, as you said, to be nothing more than a dream."

She snorted, sending a small puff of smoke over the edge of the ledge. The smoke drifted away lazily at first until a crosswind tore it apart. "However, from my point of view this world has been my home for a few thousand years. I have marked the passing of time with my youth, conflict and avoidance of humans, the discovery of what is now my home, and found a mate for my first clutch of eggs."

Her gaze was patient and level with my own. "If this world is nothing more than a dream, then the dreamer has been asleep for a very, very long time and I do not wish them to ever wake. This world feels very, very real to me, and I see nothing around to make me change this perception. Other than you."

That wasn't the answer I expected. I stifled a yawn and said, "So then, if this world isn't a dream, how am I here?"

"That is a good question. How do you transverse between worlds?"

"Transverse?"

"Cross. How do you go from one to the other?"

"Ah." I shrugged. "I have no idea. I go to sleep in my world and wake up here. When I go to sleep here, I wake up back there."

"Hmm." Cerridwen watched me stifle another yawn. "Sleep will be coming to you soon, will it not?"

"Yes. And a Worker can fall asleep quickly. We aren't allotted a lot of time for sleep, so you learn to take it when you get it." I looked upwards, my gaze resting on some clouds rolling lazily by. "I could lie down now and be asleep in a few minutes. Why?"

"I will watch as you fall asleep, to see what happens. Earlier, you appeared out of nowhere against that tree, and curiosity kept me there long enough for you to wake. Now I'm curious to see what happens when you fall asleep."

I nodded. "Sounds reasonable. But where..."

"There is plenty of room against the walls leading to my home's entrance, I'd suggest there. You wouldn't want to fall asleep near the edge of the precipice, I don't think."

"Ah, no." She had a very valid point. I moved over and propped myself up against the wall close to her tunnel entrance. "So... just go to sleep, and you'll tell me when I return what happens?"

"Yes."

"Alright." I closed my eyes. It wasn't long before I felt the edges of sleep approaching. "Wait." I opened my eyes again and looked at Cerridwen. "I almost forgot. Thank you."

"For what?" The dragon's voice was curious.

"For showing me all this. The land from the sky. Your home. Your children. Explaining some of this world to me. All of it. I... I thank you."

"As I said, Mark, you are unlike any human I've ever met." She studied me for a long moment before bowing her head, once. With her eyes still carefully watching me, she continued, "And you're welcome. Now sleep."

"Will do." I closed my eyes again, this time surrendering to the iron grip of sleep.

CHAPTER TWELVE – SUBTLE AWAKENINGS

There were still a few minutes left before the blaring of the work siren, but I found myself staring at my drab ceiling. I had been awake now for close to an hour – a very unusual prospect for me. Normally my sleep was completely uninterrupted until the siren sounded, then I would be up and moving as fast as every other Worker.

Granted, lately my nights had not been uninterrupted sleep cycles by any fashion. As I lay on my bed slab, counting the cracks in the ceiling, it occurred to me I was... disappointed? Disappointed by the fact I'd woken up to grey concrete and plaster, a drab room with nothing inside but the absolute essentials. Disappointed by my life, perhaps?

These were dangerous thoughts. A Worker did not question his life. But here I was, doing that very thing, and all because of a continual dream? Silly.

Silly? Was it?

This was the only life I'd ever known. The only life any of us had ever known. You did not question it. But yet...

Question. That's what I was doing, wasn't it? I was questioning things. Who I was. What I was doing, my lot in life, my life itself, and everything in it. All dangerous, possibly lethal thoughts. Thankfully, just thoughts. Thoughts couldn't be detected by the Corporation yet, at least not that I knew of.

If I spoke out, of course, then it'd be a lengthy time in deprogramming and mind wiping. I'd be lucky if I remembered how to walk upright without drooling, much less speak of dreams and disappointment.

But. But... but... but... That other place was too alluring. What if it was real? Cerridwen had raised some pretty solid points. None of which, of course, explained remotely how I managed to be in my world at one moment and her world the next, which was beyond frustrating.

I sat up and sighed, shaking my head to try to clear my thoughts. A robotic voice intoned, "Need?"

I replied, "Food. Water."

There was a pause, then "... Granted. Wakeup alarm in 3.24 minutes."

I muttered, "Well, I can eat early, that's something. I'm starving." I made my way over to the table as my mush arrived with a clank. Perhaps it was the influence from the other world getting to me, but the thought of eating the food paste today turned my stomach.

But I was too hungry to turn it away and the reality of trying to work on an empty stomach won out, and I shoveled it down with a grimace before I headed out the door. I was standing in the rain even before the first alarm claxon sounded for people to wake; so for a short time, I was completely alone at the bus stop as the dingy rain did what it could to soak me to the bone.

I shook my head in wry amusement. This rain was pathetic, almost nothing compared to what I'd woken up to in my dream world. I looked up into the rain and muttered, "Oh, you're going to have to do better than that, my friend..."

"Hmm?" The new guy looked rather astonished as he approached. "My word, is that an honest to God smile on your face, Worker?"

If it was, it was immediately replaced by a frown. I glared in his direction and turned away.

"Still nothing to say to me today, huh?" The new guy slid up next to me and stood just far enough away that he wasn't in my personal space, but close enough that I was very well aware of his presence.

I glared at him. "This whole waiting area with no one but us two here yet, and you have to be right next to me?"

"Correct." He peered at me. "Wait. You look different than you did the other day."

"What?" I blinked. "How... how so?"

"You're darker. Like you've been out in the sun a lot. How are you getting a tan?"

"A tan? What's that?"

"Where your skin gets darker because of exposure to excessive sunlight."

Excessive sunlight? Well, three suns would give off more than excessive sunlight, I assumed. I shrugged. Might as well tell the truth. "Probably where I was riding on the back of Cerridwen the dragon while I was sleeping last night. Those three suns are pretty bright, you know." I motioned toward the earth. "Or maybe from the hot lava we were working near yesterday? A side effect from something that got in my suit from one of the Pipes? Or you're just imagining it?"

"Oh. Yeah, I'm just probably just seeing things." After another close look at me, the new guy shook his head and dropped the subject, thankfully. The rest of the time waiting for the bus passed without incident as the remainder of the team arrived in rank and file.

But then, it happened. The bus, as usual, was late. We arrived nearly a full hour late to the assignment, and as normal, the Boss was furious with us. He was so mad, he was pacing by the bus stop even before we got off the bus. The screaming was going to be intense, you could tell... the veins in his head were already pressing for release before he'd uttered a single word.

We were all loathe to move off the bus; all but the new guy. He was in motion even before the bus came to a stop and was out the door the moment it cracked open. The Boss's mouth began to open, but the new guy met him mid-yell and out-shouted him in the finest example of bravado I'd ever seen.

I don't know what the new guy said to the Boss. The screeching of the bus's brakes and the surprised murmurs from the collected Workers pretty much drowned out any chance I had at hearing what might have been said, especially given that I was close to the back of the bus. By the time I managed to file out of the bus and took my place in line, the yelling was done and new guy was standing at his designated spot all well and neat with a satisfied look on his face.

The Boss simply looked flustered and deflated.

No yelling. No threats. No nothing.

This was... odd.

You didn't counter authority, even as minor an authority as the Boss. That would equate to a mind wipe at best, and at worst, well... swimming in a pool of lava wasn't for the faint of heart. But here the new guy was, only a few days in, and he'd just rendered the Boss ineffective in our eyes.

Maybe... maybe it was my experiences with my dreams talking, but I was beginning to see things in a new, clearer light.

I peered at the new guy with a hard look as the claw descended to take us to our job location, and a thought crossed my mind. Maybe it was time to actually listen to him. See what it was he'd been trying to tell me these past couple of days. I didn't have to act upon anything he suggested, after all... just listen.

No harm in just listening. Right?

CHAPTER THIRTEEN – STIRRING THE POT

Something amazing was happening. In all my years of riding the bus to and from the Pipes, I'd never once heard any inane chatter coming from the Workers. Not once. No idle gossip, nothing more than an occasional hushed whisper here and there. But after that display today, the bus was abuzz with whispers and murmurs, with more than an occasional sidelong glance at the new guy. I, of course, did my best to avoid his gaze. He was sitting directly across from me, his eyes peering toward mine as he tried in vain to catch my eye with every opportunity.

It might be time to listen, but not yet, not right this second, not right now, dammit! Not with all these people around! Too much too soon too fast too... too everything!

"You don't like me much, do you?" The phrase was low, barely above a whisper, but just loud enough for my hearing. I moved my gaze up and stared at the man before me, meeting his eyes finally. "I'm not asking you to accept me as a person, or a friend. But just to hear me out as a human being." After a moment, he added, "... please."

Fine. Fricking frackin' forget it. Fine. "Fine. After the bus drops us off and everyone else has returned home, we'll talk. Until then, be quiet."

"Will do." The new guy lapsed into silence, staring out through the grimy mess of a window into the outside world – at least as best as he could.

After the other passengers' conversations had died down, it occurred to me that I couldn't keep just calling him the 'new guy.' Certainly he must have a name, having come from the upper reaches of the City and all, right?

I cleared my throat, and he looked at me with a raised eyebrow. "So, ah, what do you want me to call you?"

"You mean, my name?"

"Well, I suppose. Yeah. Your name."

"Allen." He nodded in my direction. "Yours?"

"Mark."

"Good to meet you, Mark."

"You know that's a lie."

"Maybe. Maybe not."

We lapsed back into silence again. The bus rumbled and grumbled its way to our hovels, vomiting us out without ceremony to allow us to shamble back home, to start the cycle anew once again on the morrow. A never changing cycle that we never questioned.

Yet here I was, standing by the new guy... by Allen, I corrected myself... standing by Allen as the rest of my team shuffled off to their homes. Once everyone was out of earshot, I sighed and slumped my shoulders. "Well, go ahead. Talk."

"I'll make this quick, since I doubt you want any sugar coating."

"Any what?"

"Exactly." Allen paused, and then asked, "Are you happy here?'

"Are you kidding?" I shook my head. "None of us are. It's not our lot in life to be happy. It's our lot to work, that's it."

"You're wrong." Allen motioned up. "Up there, in the actual City, people are allowed to be who they want to be. There is some hierarchy, to be sure, and money plays a big part of it, but you still have a lot of individual freedoms that are inherent, no matter who you are."

"That's a lot of words that don't make sense." I shook my head. "No one down here is allowed to be who they want to be. Nothing down here would WORK if that was the case."

"You don't know that." Allen crossed his arms and leaned up against a nearby pole. "We have industry up above, same as down here. Not quite as dangerous, maybe, but we have it all the same. The more dangerous stuff, we have machines to do for us; not people."

"That's stupid. Machines can't react like a human can, can't weld with precision like..." I paused with the realization that I was simply reciting the mantra the Corporation had fed us all from a young age. "Well... anyway. Even if you're right, what exactly do you think I can do? I'm a Worker."

"Exactly."

I rubbed my temples. Talking to this man was making my head hurt. "So... you want me to fix their pipes?"

"No." Allen smiled. "But you are a Worker. And so is everyone else down here. And if everyone down here stops working, no one does any work. All work stops..."

"No... work... happens." I felt the color drain from my face as the dreaded words etched their way past my lips. "That... god... the Corporation would be FURIOUS!"

"Indeed. And then they'd have to listen."

"They'd kill us!"

"No, they wouldn't."

"Why wouldn't they?" This man was insane. That's all there was to it. He was worse than Joe. Joe at least only wanted to kill himself. This man was going to get us all killed. "You stop all work, and they'll..."

"If they kill everyone, then there will be no one left to do the work. And there wouldn't be anyone to do the work for a very long time. Everything up top would shut down for a very long time, and the Corporation wouldn't stand for that. They wouldn't like being held accountable for that." Allen motioned to the tiny shacks we lived in. "How long did you say it took to train everyone?"

"Years." The realization dawned on me like the three suns from my dream world. He was right. They couldn't kill us. They couldn't afford to. That was why they needed us mindless, complacent, obedient. I shook my head. It was too much to take in. "Alright, I can at least see your point, but I'm not ready to agree to something like that. Not now."

"I wouldn't expect you to, not that fast." Allen motioned to the hovels again. "Nor do I expect them to agree to anything with a single conversation. All I ask is for people to agree to listen, and to think. Nothing more. The world will change when it changes, nothing more nothing less."

"Well, we have spent enough time today." I turned and began to walk back to my hovel, Allen falling in step beside me. "We might miss the night meal."

"Just ask for a late meal. They'll give it to you without question. I asked for one last night just to see if they'd give me one, and they did."

"Really?" Huh. I'd never thought to even question the allotted times for meals. And here this new guy shows up and just challenges every aspect of our lives without a second thought. Maybe there was something to what he was saying.

We parted ways without any further conversation. As I expected, upon entering my home, my food had already been cleaned up. I had my clothes cleaned and my shower completed automatically, then I decided to test Allen's theory.

I cleared my throat and, without waiting for the robotic voice to respond, I said, "Request. Evening meal." I started in surprise when I heard the affirmative response.

Allen was right. My request for a meal was granted immediately. It was as unappetizing as all the other meals prior to it, but a meal it was. That, admittedly, brought up more questions than answers, but still.

The day done, it was time to sleep which was quickly becoming my favorite part of the day. As I drifted off, Allen's words echoed a few times in the back of my head.

Perhaps he was right. It might have been the experiences I'd been having in my dreams influencing my thoughts, but I was definitely starting to feel that I was being wronged with my treatment in life.

But to stop work, as a Worker? It was unheard of.

What... what would happen?

CHAPTER FOURTEEN – DREAM TO REALITY

My sleep that night was troubled. In my dreams, I saw Joe standing in front of the bus and his death replayed over and over in my mind. I heard his voice, that horrible crack in his cackling voice as he stepped out to his demise, the screech of the brakes on the bus and the crunch as Joe vanished underneath it. But through it all, I heard Joe's voice punch through, saying a simple phrase... "The clouds, Mark... the clouds."

The voice dimmed as my dream ebbed away. I slowly woke to a very comfortable feeling of warmth, my eyes cracked opened to a brilliant blue sky. Twin suns blazed away, warming the world with their energy as they patiently waited for their brethren to make his way up from the Eastern ridgeline. I yawned and stretched, careful of my surroundings as it looked like I was still in the mountains by Cerridwen's cave.

"Ah. You're awake." Cerridwen had been true to her word. She was in the exact same spot she'd been in when I'd gone to sleep, though she'd moved her head a few yards to find a more comfortable rock to lie against. "Would you like to know what I observed, Mark?"

"Yes, please." I yawned and stretched, standing up as I did so. "But give me a moment. I had some odd dreams that I need to shake out and clear my head before I try to do any deep thinking."

Cerridwen peered at me closely. "You had dreams?"

"Yeah." I moved over closer to the edge of the precipice and dangled my legs off the ledge. I gazed down to the world below and continued, "It was about one of the Workers I knew. He killed himself right before I started coming here. Kinda weird, because I'm not really one to dream much, but since I started dreaming about this world, I've been dreaming other things more often as well. It's really strange."

"Mark, think about it." Cerridwen moved to peer over the ledge beside me. She released another puff of smoke, letting the crosswind tear it apart. It seemed to amuse her.

"What do you mean?"

Cerridwen said, "You were asking me just yesterday whether this world I live in was real or a dream, correct?"

I nodded.

"You have the answer to your question, Mark. About an hour ago, there was nothing in the space where you were just now. Just rocks, a bit of grass, and air. Then, without any warning, you appeared. And last night, as you slumbered, about an hour after you went to sleep, the same thing. One moment you were there, and then you were not."

Cerridwen shifted slightly so she could see me better. "This world is no dream, my friend. No more so than your own world is a dream to me. And though I don't know or understand how, when you sleep, you somehow move between these worlds."

I frowned. "I still don't see..."

"You said you dreamed of your friend, yes?"

I nodded.

"This dream. Was it cohesive? Were your surroundings precise and solid? Was everything around you exact and factual?" Cerridwen closed her eyes and looked up toward the suns, letting the warmth of the stars soak into her face. "Talking to creatures you're not necessarily used to talking to notwithstanding of course."

"Ah." I thought for a moment, and realized she was right. This couldn't be a dream. The dream with Joe had definitely been a dream. Plenty of the qualities of it had been off. Like, at one point, I was pretty sure Joe's voice had been talking to me long after he'd been reduced to just a smear against the ground, which I was fairly confident isn't something one can do.

The dream with Joe had been disjointed, it had jumped from point to point randomly, and it even repeated itself pretty routinely. Nothing I had done in this world had been disjointed, been repeated, or anything of the sort. Everything in this world had been a fantastical version of "normal" as I could expect from reality.

The curious thing was the fact that I dreamed at all. Most nights, I was so exhausted that my sleep was deep. If I had any dreams, I slept so hard I never remembered them. Perhaps with everything that happened yesterday, my mind was just too active to slip too far into sleep? I did not know. But since the first time I'd awoken here, I'd started dreaming more often. What that meant, I did not know.

But whatever that meant, I now realized that this world MUST be real. One hundred percent, fully functioning how in the Corporation did I get here REAL. That didn't scare me, mind you. Oh no. No, not at all.

But now that I understood that this world was as real as my own world, I was filled with the desire to never, ever return to my own world. But if every time I slept I switched worlds, how could I avoid it?

I sighed and slumped my shoulders. Cerridwen said gently, "Though it was amusing to watch those emotions play out on your face, my friend, I can tell something is bothering you. Are you alright?"

"I... yeah, I'm ok. You're right. This..." I waved my hand absently, "... this all, all of this, it's all real. You, all of this, it all has to be real. I mean, that's not a bad thing, not at all, but man, this really is a lot to take in, you know?"

"I know, my friend. I know, and I'm sorry."

"Don't be sorry." I smiled half-heartedly. "What do you have to be sorry for? That you're real? That's a silly thing to be sorry for."

"Perhaps, but I'm sorry that you're having to go through all of this. As I said, you're quite different from any human I've ever heard about." Cerridwen looked off into the distance for a long moment. "Speaking of the humans, have you met any of this world's humans?"

"Beyond some odd creatures that screamed at me, you're the first living thing I've found."

"Screamed at you?"

"Yeah." I thought back, trying to think how to describe the creature. "It was this thing, about this big." I cupped my hands together and held them up for the dragon to see. "Had some form of bladed weapon on its face, claws at the end of thin bones for its legs, and wings hidden against its round body. When I got close to it, the blasted thing took to the air. Strangest thing I've ever seen. Oh, and it was blue."

"Blue, you say." There was laughter in Cerridwen's voice as the dragon tried in vain to contain her mirth. "My friend, what you described is called a bird. Specifically, a bluebird. Unless you're a bug or a seed, it's perfectly harmless."

"Ah." Nope. I'd never heard of such a thing at home, but I wasn't really sure any birds still existed. If they did, they'd live in the City side of things, and definitely not in my Undercity. "And the screaming?"

"That was it chirping, trying to find a mate, or simply being happy."

"Happy. That screech was happiness?"

"Yes."

"Huh. That's... not quite how I'd expect 'happy' to sound."

"Well, regardless." Cerridwen stood carefully and stretched, which was quite an impressive sight. "I believe it's time you met some of your kind here. I'll take you down near their home, and let you walk the rest of the way in. I doubt they'd be very welcoming if I dropped you off in the center of their homes."

"Are you sure that's wise?" I frowned. "You said yourself that I'm unlike any human you've met in this world. So by that logic, why would I get along with them?"

"Sooner or later, you're going to need to meet the humans. I'd rather it be sooner." Cerridwen sniffed the air. "It won't be too much longer before the seasons will change, and it will turn colder. Cold or hot does not matter to me, but I have no protection for you against the cold, and you would die." She turned and gazed at me. "I would prevent that as best I can."

I nodded. "Well, I could try building a shelter or something..."

Cerridwen shook her head. "This high in the mountains, it gets very cold and snows. It's warm now because of the suns and the season, but that will change. You need human shelter, and food, and warmth, and companionship. For that, you'll need their village. So I will bring you down to them, and the rest will be up to you. If you run into any trouble, just escape into the forest and I will find you."

I sighed. "Alright. Let's go."

CHAPTER FIFTEEN – EDGE OF TOWN

I watched Cerridwen take to the air with more than a fair share of trepidation. As I'd told her, until now, she'd been the only living creature I'd encountered other than... what'd she call that creature, a bird? The bird notwithstanding.

I wasn't entirely confident how I'd react around people other than Workers from my world. I mean, when it came right down to it, I wasn't exactly a wonderful specimen of humanity in my own world. Workers were trained to AVOID talking to each other, to the point we took extreme measures to not even make eye contact in the same bus.

Oh yeah. Meeting strangers in a world where I was the outsider. This was going to be simple. I wondered idly if Cerridwen remembered that I was as different to them as she would be if she came to my home? I shook my head with chagrin and, grim, decided that the only real option I had to was to get it over with.

Cerridwen hadn't wanted to get too close to the town for obvious reasons, so she'd dropped me off about a half-day's walk from the village. If they had seen her arrive or leave, they would not tie her flight to my arrival. The path to town was easily spotted from air; a road had been cut through the forest. All I had to do, essentially, was to find it, then follow it. Simple.

Granted, that involved finding said road. It was supposed to be somewhere in the direction I'd been walking. By the time I finally stumbled upon it, I'd gotten turned around a half-dozen times and backtracked another dozen times beyond that. But find the road I did, and after a moment to curse at the forest, I started off down the road.

It occurred to me as I walked how pointless my initial excursion into this world had truly been. When I'd first arrived, I'd simply picked a direction and started walking. Now, even with ample directions and guidance from having flown over the area, I'd gotten lost for half the day.

Deep in my thoughts, I hardly noticed that it was starting to grow dark when I finally came within sight of the village, and I pulled up to a stop in sheer wonder. As Cerridwen had told me, the village was, indeed, teeming with people. They numbered at least a hundred by my quick count, wandering from house to house in what looked to be some form of communal evening meal. Men and women of all ages took turns carrying trays of food to those who could not do so for themselves, removed trays that were of no use, and maneuvered with an agile grace between children that played merrily between bites of food.

This. This is what I had imagined in my deepest forbidden dreams that the sounds of "happiness" truly was. There were sounds I never even imagined I'd hear. Here was an entire village of people, of all ages, simply enjoying a meal and laughing, singing...

And being happy.

After a moment, I understood. This is what Cerridwen truly wanted me to see. Not the village itself, not the people themselves, but the true difference between what I had told her of my world and what she knew of her world.

People here were happy. They might have known hardship, strife, pain, anguish, and suffering in their time, but for the moment, they were happy. I couldn't think of a single time in my life that would qualify as being happy until coming to this world.

The realization hit me like a wrench against an empty pipe, and I steadied myself against a tree. But it was the truth. I... I truly was happy here. Here, I didn't have to consider what the Corporation expected of me. I didn't have to look over my shoulder constantly to see who was watching, to ensure I was doing what the Corporation thought I should be doing. I had an entirely new world to explore and a friend in Cerridwen to explain the ins and outs to me. And now, I had a whole town full of my own kind to...

To... to what? I frowned. What, exactly, did I really and truly expect to gain from these people? I'd been lucky with Cerridwen, I knew she could have easily killed me, and chose to not do so. What if any of these hundred or so villagers decided I wasn't worth leaving alive? I had no means to defend myself.

Frozen in indecision, I ended up standing motionless at the outskirts of the village as the day turned into night. I'd never managed to stay awake in this place long enough to see it turn fully night. I wasn't even really sure how the various cycles between here and home meshed; heck, I'd only just a few hours ago accepted that this world was real!

I truly didn't know what to do. Approaching the village terrified me more than going up to the Boss and giving him a great big hug. Cerridwen hadn't mentioned any particular methods of formal greetings. Did I just walk up and wave? Blend in and assimilate into the crowd as if I lived there and hope no one noticed?

Cerridwen.

The urge to just run away, back into the forest and wait until Cerridwen came back to find me was strong, but I resisted it. She would be quite disappointed if I didn't at least try to go into the village at least once. I didn't want to disappoint her, but it sure would be nice to have had her reassuring voice to coax me along right now.

But no, I was alone. Granted, I didn't mind being alone, even in a world as unfamiliar as this was to me, but still... this would be significantly easier if I wasn't. I sighed deeply and turned my gaze back to the village as lights began to appear from within the buildings. From the dancing, flickering nature of the lights, I assumed the light sources to be some form of flame and not the unforgiving, cold light sources from my home.

I found myself wondering what it was like for them. What life was like here? Did they have a Boss to tell them what to do? A Corporation that watched everything that they did? Or what was the word Allen had used? Freedom?

I don't know how long I sat there and watched the village fall asleep. Eventually, my legs gave out and I slumped against a nearby tree. My memories still ringing with the pleasantness of the scenes I'd witnessed, I drifted off to the first relaxed sleep I could remember in quite a long time.

CHAPTER SIXTEEN – CROSSING A DANGEROUS LINE

When I dreamed that night, my dreams were strange and disjointed. Nothing about them had any concrete form, but there was an odd feeling of loss, of sorrow, of betrayal, and of despair. But through the soup of my unconsciousness, nothing concrete formed and soon enough I was waking on my slab.

Home again, as usual. It was a full hour before I was slated to wake for the day and there I lay, flat on my back and staring up at my ceiling, contemplating trees and villages instead of sleeping. What was wrong with me?

This had to be all Joe's fault, I decided. All of this began the day Joe threw himself under the bus. His insane ramblings about clouds and the sky; somehow that must have triggered some latent... thing... inside me that led me to start...

...moving between worlds when I slept.

Yeah, that didn't sound insane at all. I shook my head and sat up. My room's robotic voice immediately said, "Need?"

I responded, "Food."

A pause, then, "Granted."

Allen had been right. There wasn't even a hesitation this time, a tray simply slid into place and my grey slop dropped into place. The same old grey mush I'd eaten twice a day, every day, since I could remember.

I had not been able to clearly see what the villagers had been eating yesterday, but it hadn't appeared to be mush of any particular color. I would have to try to get closer tomorrow for a better view. I ate my mush begrudgingly, watching with only a mild interest as my tray was whisked away to wherever it went for disposal.

Now the big question. What, exactly, was I supposed to do before I went to work? I sighed and shrugged. There wasn't anything to do here, and I wasn't about to go back to sleep, so why not just head to the bus stop and watch the world wake up? I'd never done that before. Last night I'd watched one world go to sleep, so perhaps it was time to watch my world wake.

I approached the door to my home and paused. We had been told from the day we were born that all our actions were recorded and tracked. You didn't leave your homes without prior authorization, and absolutely never before it was at least close to the time for you to leave. Right now, this? This was against authorized protocol, the Corporation should be bringing all of its powers ringing down around my ears the moment I stepped outside.

Granted, I mused... a good mind wipe might also stop me from going to the other world and let me resume my life without all this confusion. So... the dice cast, I opened the door and stepped out into the world, expecting the worst.

Nothing. Nothing occurred at all. I stood in front of my home, waiting for anything to happen for a minute or two. When it became readily apparent that we had all been lied to, I shrugged and off to the bus stop I went. Once it came into view, I blinked in surprise. Someone was already there.

Allen watched me approach with what I suspected was a smug expression. "So. Thought about what we talked about?"

"A bit."

"And?"

"I find it hard to believe that's your entire plan." I motioned to the hovels. "You have all of us Workers just stop working. Then what? The Corporation sends in their Enforcers, and we get slaughtered until whoever's left starts working again. That doesn't sound like a very well thought out plan."

"I don't think they'll risk that." Allen shook his head. "I mean, yes, there is that chance, but I don't think it's a big chance, because if they did that, they would lose so many Workers their production would tank."

"And if they did?"

"What would happen if you used your tools on someone?"

"What? Like my fusion blowtorch? That's against the Corporation guidelines..."

"Mark. We don't care what the Corporation requires, remember?"

"... oh. Right." I shook my head. "Well, my fusion blowtorch is designed to bind together any of the known metals on the planet. By the same token, it can be used to cut through the same metals. So it would split apart Enforcer armor in no time at all."

"What about the Enforcers inside the armor?"

"Oh, they'd probably boil alive in a couple of seconds. Oh. Oh, I see." It dawned on me then. Why they needed us compliant, obedient, and complacent. We could be very, very dangerous if we wanted to be. And thanks to Allen, suddenly I was thinking that perhaps, just perhaps... I wanted to be.

"Now you're catching on." Allen closed his eyes and leaned back against a pole. "One man doesn't make an army, but it is at least a start."

"I never said I'm on board." I sighed, shaking my head. "But I... I've seen some things recently that have opened my eyes to some, shall we say, possibilities that things shouldn't be the way they are. And let's just leave it at that, because it's hard to explain beyond that."

"Oh, you're on board." Allen opened one eye and peered at me. "I can see it in your expression. That look in your eyes, that pull in your shoulders, the draw in your face. You're standing straighter, there's a gleam in your gaze, and hope in your stance. Even a glimmer of change is worth risking it all, and you know it, don't you?"

I turned my back on Allen and refused to answer him for a while. I had come out here to watch the world wake up, and damn it all, that's what I was going to do.

This, unfortunately, turned out to be considerably less impressive than watching the other world go to sleep. At the exact same time as always, the alarm claxon sounded and movement could been seen in every hovel within visual range. Within a few minutes, Workers shuffled their way out the doors and to the bus stop, ready to start the day.

It was pathetic. I hated to admit it, but I was tired. Tired of it. Tired of this life. Tired of every aspect of this entire existence. I sighed and turned back to Allen. "Yes, Allen. Yes, I do know it. And against my better judgement, I am on board. So what's the next step?"

"The next step is to take one and make two. And from two, four. Four, eight. And so on, and so on, until all the Workers have at least heard." Allen stood up from the pole and stretched. "My little exercise yesterday has a lot of the other Workers talking. They know I'll stand up to at least the Boss, and I'm hoping I can leverage that to get them to stand up for themselves too before I get myself killed."

"Wait." I glanced at Allen. "So... you did that yesterday, knowing that you could very well be punished or even killed, specifically to set things up to help all of us stand up for ourselves?"

"To put it in terms a Worker would understand, you don't set a Pipe without setting a good foundation first, do you not?"

"No, no you do not." This was a bit of a surprise. Why would he do that? That didn't benefit him at all, did it? Why would...

The concept of selflessness was a new concept to me, but I was beginning to understand. I think. I wouldn't do it myself, I don't think... but would I defend Cerridwen if necessary? Yes. So then maybe I did understand. I shook my head. "You're a fool, Allen."

"Can't be sane if you want to change the world, my friend."

"Oh, well I have good news for you there. I don't think I'm sane either."

"Oh?"

"Trust me, you wouldn't believe me even if I told you."

"Try me."

"Very well. I think I move between worlds when I sleep."

"...what?"

CHAPTER SEVENTEEN – DISCOVERING MARK

The day itself was definition of mundane, which made it anything but. The Boss, after yesterday's interaction with Allen, didn't say a word to us. In all my years working for him it was a first. Not. One. Word. It was glorious, for all the ominous promise of retribution it held. Retribution or no, though, for one fantastic day, we had peace and quiet.

This, of course, gave all us Workers plenty to talk about on the ride home. The buzz on the bus was louder than yesterday, when Allen had confronted the Boss. This time, the glances toward Allen were longer, and people did not look away when he met their gaze.

More worrisome to me, though, were how many were now looking at me as well. I don't know why. I hadn't done anything to attract anyone's attention, short of talking to Allen. Though maybe they were just looking at me as a way to get through to him? I did not know.

Regardless, no one approached me as I made my way back to my home, and I breathed a sigh of relief when my day ended uneventfully. Now it was nearly time to sleep, and I was bound and determined to see if I could get closer to that village.

My excitement nearly kept me from sleeping, but years of conditioned patterns as a Worker helped me drop off into deep sleep nearly the moment I laid down on my slab, my grey mush untouched on the table.

My dreams that night were disjointed again. There was a family, though I could not see the faces or figures clearly enough to make out any details. But there were clearly parental figures, with children, stand-

85

ing by a table. Through the fog of my dreams, a hand reached out to sign a document. With the signing of the document, the sounds of a closing door, a feeling of loss, hopelessness... then the dream faded, and the emptiness returned.

In the darkness of my slumber, I began to hear a murmuring. It was low, barely audible, but enough to register in my subconscious. I grimaced and began to awaken, realizing as I did so that the sound I was hearing was voices. Voices meant someone was coming near my home, and that meant possibly Enforcers?

Enforcers? Enforcers! I bolted upright, the thought jolting me out of my sleep in a cold sweat.

"Easy, son, easy." The voice was cracked, weathered and beaten, but gentle in its tone. "We aren't going to hurt you, boy, settle down."

"What?" I blinked, slowly coming to the realization I was in the other world again. Finally, I relaxed and shook my head, clearing my thoughts. The Enforcers weren't here. I was safe, at least from them. I turned and looked to see whom had spoken.

"You alright there, son?" The man asked in a voice that creaked and cracked as it carefully pulled its way through the air. I got a good look at him this time, and his appearance reflected his voice appropriately. The man was of an advanced age, older than any Worker I'd ever known by far. His hair had vanished entirely save small tufts of white wiry bits around his ears. His forehead and face were heavily wrinkled and covered with pockmarks, but his eyes twinkled with kindness and his mouth was creased in a well-used smile. He walked with a limp and a cane. He would never have survived back home, yet obviously here that wasn't the case.

His clothing was odd. Back home, everything had a purpose; the form-fitting work suit was designed to give at least partial protection against whatever element we Workers were exposed to, and to help seal against toxins. The loose-fitting cloak the man wore against his absently-tossed on robes looked almost like an afterthought for his day's regime. A few pouches were scattered haphazardly around a length of cord across his chest, and though his clothes were obviously well worn from travel, he wore no shoes on his feet.

His companion stood a good head and shoulders taller than the older man, and was nearly twice as broad. Whereas the elder man was dressed almost haphazardly, this man's garb was almost pristine. His thin shirt and knee-length pants strained against barely-restrained muscles. I'd never seen a man this muscular before, and his bulk was rather astonishing. This man was dragging a large amount of some plant behind him with his muscular arms, and was looking at me through his blonde curls with an idle curiosity. He had not spoken yet.

"I... yes. I am fine." I brushed myself off idly and glanced around. Other than these two men, no one else was nearby. They didn't appear to be threatening. "I'm sorry, was this your tree I was sleeping against?"

"Nah." The bigger man spoke this time, his voice a surprisingly higher pitched, nasally tone. He motioned with a rather large paw toward the tree I'd been slumbering against dismissively. "Isn't no one's tree. But why are you sleeping now? Been suns-up for hours."

"Suns up?" The term wasn't familiar. "Er, right. I..."

The older man peered at me, his eyes sharp. "Hold on a second, son. You're not from around here, are you?"

"What..." How by the Corporation could he possibly know that, so fast? "What, ah, what makes you say that?"

"You're as pale as a newborn." The man's cane snaked out and snagged my arm, pulling me toward him with little resistance on my part. "Those clothes of yours don't look nothin' like I've ever seen, and I've seen a lot, believe me." Before I realized it, I was standing within a few inches of the man's face. His scent wafted over me the moment I got close to him; it was an earthy scent, that of someone who worked the land, pleasant and inviting, not that of anything I'd smelled back home.

He inspected my face, moving onto my arms and legs next. "Skinny as a pole. You look like you haven't eaten a real meal in years. How long you've been on your own, son, a decade?"

The bigger man nodded, crossing his arms as he watched the inspection. "Pale as a ghost too. Guessing that's intentional. Smart moves on your part."

"I... I'm afraid I don't... understand." It was quite difficult to talk with the older man pulling on my clothing, arms and legs. Just keeping my balance was taking most of my concentration Workers didn't really have any privacy to speak of, but this just... didn't quite feel right.

The big man motioned upwards. "The suns sap your energies way too fast, so best t' travel when it's dark. When it's suns up, stay under shade and keep cool. Don't know if you meant to, but that's what it looks like you did. Smart to do it that way."

"Um... ow, that hurt, stop that... well, it wasn't... intentional?" I'm sure I sounded really convincing. No Enforcer would be fooled by my feeble attempts at lying, and I doubted these two would either. "Honestly, I'm not even sure where I am."

"You're close to the town of Syniar." This was said matter-of-fact by the older man. "We're a fringe town, edge of civilization type of thing. Not a lot to our home, we're a farming and lumber town for the most part. We don't get a lot of visitors, so as long as you're here on peaceful intentions, you being here's a cause for a celebration."

"Farming and lumber." These words were foreign. And what was a celebration? That sounded dangerous. "Definitely peaceful, and ah, I don't think I want a 'celebration.' That doesn't sound..."

"Nonsense." The old man finished inspecting me head to toe and pushed himself back up to a standing position. "I won't hear it. Everyone loves a good party, and we've needed an excuse for a good one for a while now. Plus, you look like you haven't had anything to eat but sticks and bugs for months, so the extra food will do you good. Put some meat back on those bones of yours."

The man was talking faster than a riveter could attach a pipe. I could barely follow along, much less understand what he was talking about. I simply nodded my head absently like a child's doll. Still talking, the older man walked off to the road, heading in what I assumed was the direction of the village.

I surmised I was to follow along. I was about to do so when a rather large hand gave me pause by gripping my shoulder. I turned my head and gazed into the calm eyes of the other man who'd found me.

He, too, took a quick look of me up and down, and he frowned. "Know this, stranger. I have my eye on you. I don't know you, and I don't necessarily trust you as of yet." He motioned to the tree where I'd awoken. "Where do you hail from?"

I saw no real particular reason to lie. I shrugged and replied, "From the Undercity."

"From the what?"

"The Undercity. I'm a Worker for the Corporation, and I've lived my whole life in the Undercity."

The man stared at me long and hard for a minute before he finally split his face in a grin. "Alright. Since you can't tell me the truth, I'll just keep BOTH eyes on you!" He released the plants he'd been dragging behind him and, with almost no effort at all, picked me up into the air and carried me along as he walked behind the older man. With his other hand, he picked back up the plants and continued to drag them behind him

To my chagrin, I yelped in surprise as he picked me up. "But... but that was the truth!"

"Yeah, and I'm a centidragon!"

"What's a centidragon?"

"You'll meet one in town. Come on, let's catch up to Foa, for an old man he's quick, and if he gets home too far ahead of me, Iri will never let me hear the end of it."

CHAPTER EIGHTEEN – WELCOME HOME

Once on the road, it didn't take long to reach the outskirts of the village, at least once the big man relented and put me back on the ground. As I'd surmised from the air, the plants that were in rows were that way intentionally. The villagers were moving amongst the plants, doing something to them that I did not understand, and chatting idly among themselves. A few of them waved in greeting to us, and though my companions returned the greeting, I did not.

I wasn't really sure what I was supposed to do, in the first place. I knew how to wave, but how long was too long? Too fast, too slow? I felt completely out of place here in the village, and sure as the Corporation a smile felt foreign to my face. Waving was not a good idea at all. No, better to just walk along beside these two and pretend I was back home.

I'd wanted to get closer to the village, I admit. Maybe not quite this close, quite this quickly.

The larger man, whom I'd learned was named Jun when we'd exchanged names along the road, glanced down at me and smirked. "What's wrong, Mark? Not the friendly type?"

"Uh, no. No. Friendliness isn't exactly encouraged by the Corporation."

"No kidding. I've met dragons friendlier than you."

I skidded to a halt. "You've met a dragon? Was it Cerridwen? I've been trying to figure out..."

"Easy, boy." Foa laughed. "It's an expression. Dragons are not friendly. They'd sooner eat you than anything else. That's it."

"Oh." Well, that was a disappointment. "But then... you mentioned a centidragon earlier. What's the difference?"

"Multiple thousands of pounds. A centidragon's a bit bigger than a horse. A dragon's a bit bigger than a third of the village." Jun adjusted his grip on the grasses he was pulling along behind him. After he had explained that they were for repairing the roofs of some damaged homes from the storm the other day, I was more excited than I cared to admit to the man to see this process. Plants, for a roof cover? Not steel or a plastic composite? I couldn't wait to see it in action.

He continued, "We have two of them in the village, and we use them to pull carts. They gave us an egg clutch recently, and Iri's keeping an eye on the eggs to see when they hatch."

"Why?"

"Don't rightly know. Going to see if there's any use to keeping centidragons around for any purpose."

I scratched at an itch as we walked. "What possible purpose? I mean, I don't even know what these things are. But still..."

"Well, there's a couple things they might be good for." Jun ticked them off on his fingers as he talked. "Once the eggs hatch, the centidragons could produce milk like a goat or a cow. If they do, we might be able use that milk ourselves as a food source. So that's one. For two, they make great pack animals. They don't tire nearly as fast as a horse or mule, and go much longer distances through worse weather. They require less food." He jerked a thumb over his shoulder in a vague direction, I assumed where the centidragons were housed. "They eat anything."

"Anything?"

"Yup. Rocks, sticks, bugs, leaves, you name it, I've seen them eat it. So they're easier to keep alive than horses and mules. Oh, and though we haven't tried it yet, in a pinch we can probably eat them too. So that's three things."

Jun sneezed. "Ugh, sorry about that. There's also a large amount of money to be made from raising centidragons if we can do it right. Their scales and tail can sell for a considerable sum as alchemy ingredients, and they're pretty rare in most parts of the world. They're all over the place out here, so even if we can't raise them, we can still hunt for them."

I was about to respond when a shrill voice cut through the air. A mass of blonde curly hair shot through my field of vision and sprang into the air. The person attached to the blonde hair dived into Jun's arms with gusto, laughing with a high-pitched glee. She was dressed remarkably similar to the large man, though her clothes were not nearly as form-fitting. "Jun!"

"Heyya, sis." Jun returned her flying hug with a good-natured one of his own, placing her back on the ground. "Careful with those flying leaps, Iri. You nearly ran over Mark here."

"Mark?" The young woman turned and looked at me, and I found myself looking into the eyes of the first woman I'd ever seen up close. Her eyes were a striking blue, nearly as blue as the skies above. They met mine with a steadiness I'm sure I couldn't match, and I quickly turned my gaze away, uneasy. "Oh! Hello!"

"Um. Yes. Hello." I shifted on my feet. I didn't like this close of attention, at all. People paying attention to me in general made me uncomfortable. This woman was... something else.

"So what's your story?" Iri leaned up against her brother while fixing me with that unsettling gaze of hers. "Lost traveler? Runaway soldier? Nice outfit."

Jun snorted. "No, claims he's from someplace called the 'Undercity.' Works for something called the 'Corporation.' Ever heard of either?"

"Nope. Doesn't mean it doesn't exist. Maybe in one of the cities across the sea?" Iri shrugged. "Either way, welcome to our home, Mark. I'll go let the other town elders know. I hope you're hungry."

"Hungry?" I considered for a moment. My stomach answered for me with an audible growl, and I sighed sheepishly. It had been quite a while since my last food paste. "Well, I suppose I can always eat..."

"Good. They'll stuff you so full of food you'll pop. I'll be off then." Iri waved goodbye to Jun and danced off into the village, where a crowd was gathering. Apparently word had already spread that Jun and Foa had not returned alone. People were moving into groups to see us and talking amongst themselves.

Milling about, talking freely, laughing and enjoying themselves. Such an alien concept to even consider. Back home, this would not have been allowed in any way, shape, or fashion. Yet another way this world was inherently alien from my own.

Foa snorted in mock derision. "That girl. In and out like a windstorm. Not even a hello for me. I'll have to pop her for that later." He brandished his walking stick threateningly.

Jun smirked. "You know as well as I do that's a bad idea."

"Yeah. She'd flatten me."

As the two of them continued to converse idly, I drifted back a bit to observe the town. The townspeople greeted Jun and Foa as we passed, with more than few curious and concerned looked my way. A few words from Foa, though, and the people usually looked away.

Usually. A few continued staring at me until we'd long since moved on past them, making me feel completely out of place.

I sighed. This place was like nothing I'd ever imagined. Up close, the buildings were, as I'd assumed, living quarters but not tiny like every one I'd ever seen. These were massive. You could fit twenty, maybe thirty people in these homes without people lying on top of each other. And if you did stack them, why, you could fit four to six times that amount. It's a wonder the Corporation hadn't thought of something like this.

And the spacing between houses left me bewildered. It made no logical sense. Twenty to forty or more strides to reach the next building was inefficient. This village took up probably eighty-five percent more land space than it needed to use than if it had just stacked things properly.

The sheer strangeness of it was making me seriously question whether I truly wanted to stay after all. Could I really adjust to this different world? But as I drifted with my thoughts, the laughter of the village's children reached my ears. The gentle sounds of the townspeople's chatter as they went about their daily business, unconcerned with a Corporation, uncaring about Enforcers, unknowing about my world entirely.

A world like that... yes. I could try to actually be truly happy here. I'd be a fool to pass up an opportunity like that.

Before I could continue my thoughts, I realized that I'd lost sight of both Jun and Foa. I frowned and started casting about, trying to find them. Jun was a huge man, how could I lose a man of that size? But sure enough, neither he nor the old man were anywhere in sight, and I was alone in sea of people I didn't know.

I turned to leave, panic setting in, when I felt a hand slide into mine. Mid-step, I turned and found myself face to face with blue eyes and curls again, and I was at a pause, completely unable to complete my step.

"Mark?" Iri smiled at me. "We lost you. That's easy to do, those two tend to prattle on and forget the world, and you're new here. Want me to show you where to go?"

Why could I suddenly not breathe? Unable to respond, I simply nodded. Still unable to find my voice, I silently let Iri guide me through the village.

CHAPTER NINTEEN – BROKEN WALLS

The chorus of calls were deafening. Iri had led me right to the center of the village where they'd been gathering for a meal. Almost immediately upon seeing this new person to the village, the questions had started in a barrage of sound. The older man had been right; apparently new people just didn't come to this village very often, so my coming was definitely a curiosity.

Iri had tried to guide me to a seat by one of the large tables, but I found that I was unable to fully sit down before I was standing up again to try to answer people's questions. But that's when I learned something. There's feeling out of place; then there's an entire village staring at me as I'm standing in front of them staring right back, trying vainly to come up with something, anything to say, really, that they might expect me to say. Glumly, after a long moment, I started to ease myself back down in my seat.

"No, wait!" To my right, Iri stood up from where she'd been seated. She turned and smiled at the gathering villagers. "This is Mark." She flashed me a grin before she continued, "He's supposed to be from somewhere called the Corporation?"

I shook my head. I tried to speak, but I'd gotten flustered by that grin from Iri and my voice just simply refused to work. That was odd. It had never done that before. But, with all the eyes on me, I was feeling odd. I went to speak again, and after a very unmistakable squeak, I managed to say, "N... no. No, I'm from the Undercity. The Corporation owns everything and runs everything, from the Undercity below to the City and above. And I live in the Undercity, which is underneath everything, down near the lava. That's why it's called the Undercity, because it's under the City."

"Oh." Iri stared at me. After a moment, her face broke into a smile as people around us started to talk again.

A voice from the crowd shouted, "Where's this Undercity at? Is it to the East?"

"Um. No. I don't think so, anyway."

"So West then?"

"I don't... I don't know."

"How do you not know?"

"I don't... it's hard to explain." It occurred to me that maybe, just maybe, I really shouldn't tell an entire village that I was going to vanish when I fell asleep tonight. I doubted it would go over very well.

The questions continued, but they were quickly drowned out by the arrival of the food. As I'd witnessed from my watching roost yesterday, villagers arrived with trays loaded down with colorful assortments of various items that I did not recognize. Each tray was delivered to a waiting recipient, who dug in with thankful gusto.

Iri flashed me another smile – she seemed to do that a lot - and handed me a tray when one of the villagers got within arm's reach of her. I nodded at her and looked down at the tray.

Not a trace of grey paste. Not a trace of any color paste. I didn't recognize anything at all! What... what was this stuff? I tentatively picked up one of the items on the tray and almost immediately put it back down. It was hot.

Jun, who had sat down on my left when he'd arrived, motioned to the tray with an object in his hand. A similar object was on my tray as well. "Most of that stuff is hot, Mark. Be careful with it or you'll burn yourself."

"Oh... Uh, thanks." I snuck a glance at the object he was holding and how he was holding it, and looked back at the tray. So this thing here. Alright. I picked up the device and gingerly balanced it between my fingers. It seemed unwieldly. After a few tries, however, I was able to scoop something and bring it up enough that I was able to smell it suspiciously.

My eyes widened with surprise. I had never smelled anything so good before! This actually smelled like something I wanted to eat. I looked at the object in my hand with trepidation. This wasn't mush. It'd been a very long time since I'd eaten solid food, but it couldn't be that much different from food paste, right?

Without any further debate, I tossed the food into my mouth and chewed enthusiastically.

That turned out to be one heck of a mistake.

The food was still hot, for one, as Jun had tried to warn me. It burned my mouth almost the moment it hit flesh. When I gagged and swallowed out of reflex, the hard and mostly unchewed mass tried to merrily make its way down my throat. This trip was sadly interrupted, and I found myself severely lacking in air.

I stood up, my throat burning and my lungs trying in vain to grasp air, any air, but finding none. The world around me narrowed in vision sharply as I tried to pull air in. There was noise around me, but I couldn't focus enough to understand any of it.

I took a step, mindless of the world around me, my panicked thoughts just wanting to try to find help. I was aware of people around me shouting, and a part of my consciousness registered that someone had shouted out that I was choking.

I felt a presence behind me as strong arms wrapped themselves around my torso. Large hands clasped themselves somewhere near my center, and I felt a thumb resting against my stomach.

With a violent jerk, whomever was behind me pulled back and up, forcing a large amount of pressure into what little stomach I had. It was more than sufficient to send the piece of food flying out of my mouth and sailing off past the other diners. I gulped and gasped for air, suddenly grateful for such a simple process.

With water welling up in my eyes making it hard to see, I fell to my knees, still gasping. I could finally hear the voices clearly again, including the voice behind.

Jun said, "You alright there, Mark?"

I rasped, "Y... yes. Yes. I am... alright." Shaky, I pulled myself back upright and carefully straightened my clothing. "What... what happened?"

"What happened?" Jun snorted. "You tossed a whole chunk of stew in your mouth is what happened."

I gagged again, the feeling of choking still present despite the fact I could breathe just fine now. "I'm sorry, I just... I..." I shook my head, trying to clear my thoughts.

"Mark?" Iri stood up and moved over to me, her hand lightly touching my arm. She looked at me with concern, examining my face as she continued, "What's wrong? You ok?"

"I..." I sighed. I couldn't take it anymore. I had to tell them the truth, or they were going to think something was really wrong with me. They weren't going to believe me. Why would they? But I couldn't lie. I just wasn't very good at it. "I... I'm not from here."

Iri's voice was gentle as she said, "We know that."

"No, I mean, I'm not from here. As in, your world." I motioned around me. "This world, with the three suns, and the trees, and you people, and Cerridwen... all of you, none of you. I'm not from here. My home is the Undercity, underneath the City, on the planet Earth."

"Cerridwen?" Iri cocked her head to the side with curiosity. "Earth? What are those?"

"I can't explain it." I sat down on the ground, acutely aware of how the conversation was very rapidly coming to a stop around me. "But they're not here. The Undercity isn't East, or West, or anywhere. It's not here. None of my home is here. And come tonight, I won't be here, either."

"Meaning?" Foa was paying attention as well, but the old man's tone wasn't threatening. He had turned his chair around and was listening politely, eating as I talked.

"Meaning that," I pointed down at the ground. "I'm here. When I go to sleep..." I moved my finger up to point at the sky, "I will wake there, home. When I go to sleep there," I returned my finger to the ground, "I'll be back here. I'm always back in the same spot I was when I left, but time has passed. I don't know how to explain it other than that."

I sighed deeply. "And I don't know why. Or how. Or most importantly, why me. I'm just a Worker. I fix pipes. That's all I do. That's all I've ever wanted to do, at least until I met Cerridwen, and then Allen, and now you folks." I pulled my knees in close, trying to make myself as small as possible.

"Hey, now, don't be that way." Iri gently put her hands over my knees, her eyes searching mine. "I'm sure there's a reason you started coming here. And you can't just be a simple Worker, whatever that is, right?"

"... why not?"

"Well... because you're here. A simple Worker wouldn't be here, now would he?"

"Uh." Huh. What an odd woman. What an odd question. And what an odd, roundabout way to be absolutely, one hundred percent right.

CHAPTER TWENTY – TWO WORLDS COLLIDE

They didn't believe me, of course. Why should they? No one just disappears when they fall asleep. I had talked a bit off and on the rest of the afternoon, trying to explain some of what I was talking about. But how to explain what I didn't even know myself?

I hadn't tried to eat again. That... stew, I think Jun called it. The stew remained on the tray, uneaten, along with whatever else was beside it. I was hungry to the point of being ravenous, but hunger was quelled by the fear of choking again. It was tough, though... It smelled good, better than anything I'd smelled in my entire life, but I just couldn't bring myself to try and eat any of it.

Iri and Jun showed me through the rest of the village after that, but most of the day became a blur. I was too embarrassed by my near-death experience and too nervous to be very comfortable with my surroundings. Iri, it seemed, could sense my discomfort, and often shot me a comforting glance or would squeeze my hand in reassurance. It... was not unwanted.

It wasn't until a creature arrived pulling a wagon that I came to a dead stop. The creature bore a rather striking resemblance to Cerridwen, at least in the head and neck area. Its head was serpentine and covered in scales, though whereas Cerridwen's had been a dark grey, this creature's scales were more brownish-green. The creature was also vastly smaller, only standing about three feet taller than I. Where Cerridwen's body had been lean and angled for flight, this creature was stocky and wingless, muscled for ground movement.

Oh, and the eight legs it bore were a considerable difference from Cerridwen as well, of course.

Jun smirked and motioned toward the creature. "Told you you'd meet a centidragon. Want to go see her?"

I hesitated. "I wouldn't mind talking to her, just not... not right now. Does she know Cerridwen?"

"Oh, she doesn't talk, Mark. Centidragons are just working animals. She'll make some clicking and purring noises if she likes you, but that's about it." Iri cocked her head quizzically. "You've mentioned that name a few times. Cerridwen. Who is that?"

I remembered something Cerridwen had told me about the other humans she'd met in this world, and how they'd tried to kill her. Humans and dragons didn't apparently get along very well, so perhaps some discretion was in order. "Just... someone that I ran into before the village. She led me to the village, but I don't know how to find her now."

"Oh, alright." Iri smiled at me. That was quite an infectious smile. Seeing it made me feel really, really odd and I wasn't sure why. "Odd name though."

"Odd?"

"Well, yeah. She must not be from around here." She motioned to a few kids playing nearby. "That's Nai, with the spiky hair. The taller one is Kia, his brother. And the girl is Pia, their sister."

"Oh, I see." I nodded. "Jun, Iri, Nai, Pia. All of your names sound like they have three letters. Am I right?"

"Yes." Iri touched me on the shoulder. "And yours does not, right?" At my nod, she continued, "Mark. Ma, rk? Four letters, or five?"

"Four. M, a, r, k."

"Four then. Does everyone where you come from have four letters to their name?"

"No. Allen, for instance, has five to his name. Joe had three. It's really kinda random, I guess." I shrugged. "Guess it depends on whoever names you."

Jun nodded. "Larger towns are like that. Here, generations ago, one of the town founders just liked the style, and it stuck." He smiled. "Makes it easy."

My stomach growled again, and I grimaced. That time, it hurt. Soon enough, I'd be back home, I kept telling myself, and I'd be able to eat then.

Iri shot me a look. "Jun or I would be more than happy to bring you some food, Mark. Just eat it slower this time, and you should be fine."

I sighed. "It might have smelled good, but that wasn't food. Not to me, anyway." I shrugged. "Nothing on the plate looked anything like what I'm used to."

Iri stopped dead in her tracks and stared at me incredulously. "What? What is food like where you're from?"

"All Workers eat a carefully balanced food paste twice a day that's carefully regulated for caloric and vitamin intake to ensure their dietary..." I paused when I realized Iri looked completely lost. "Er, a food paste. I've eaten it twice a day since as long as I can remember."

"A food... paste." Iri looked disgusted. "Like, no form to it, just a splat of something you spread on bread?"

"What is bread?"

"By the holy." Iri clapped her hands to her mouth, horrified. "Oh you poor soul. You've never even had bread? Oh, we're going to have to fix this. Not right now, of course, you just tried to choke to death, but soon enough! Oh, we're just not going to stand..." Trailing off, she grabbed my hand and pulled me toward a rather large building toward the center of town.

"Where are we going?" The woman was unusually strong. All of the villagers here bore the same general build; that of those that worked the land, I assumed. Fit and well fed, they could easily outperform a skilled Worker in most fields of expertise. But, I doubted they knew much about swinging a wrench.

Did they even have wrenches here? My thoughts wandering, I barely noticed as Iri pulled me into the large domicile and sat me down next to two large piles of bound up plants. After a moment, I realized I was now seated inside, away from the heat of the waning day and was surrounded by a dozen people I didn't recognize. The people surrounding me were all dressed in heavy cloaks, obscuring their appearances, and a heavy scented smoke hung in the air. "Uh, hello?"

"Did you not hear a word I said?" Chiding, Iri crossed her arms and frowned at me from where leaning against the door frame. "I said, these are the village elders. By now, the whole town's heard about how you claim to disappear, and the elders want to observe it. They're going to watch you sleep, see what happens try to figure out where you go when you sleep."

"Oh." I blinked, still slightly confused. "And you're... leaving?"

"So you heard that part at least." Iri nodded. "I've never been very good with cantrips, so I'm heading back to help Jun. Sleep well, and Jun and I will see you tomorrow, alright?"

"Um, alright." I nodded at her as she left, and turned my attention back to the elders. "So, ah, I guess you have some questions?"

One of the village elders cleared their throat. "Yes, we're all very curious to see how this happens."

I peered at the hooded man who'd spoken, as the voice was very familiar. "Foa?"

Foa chuckled, removing his hood. "Yes, my boy?"

I sighed in relief. "Oh, that is you."

"Yes, Mark. Did I forget to mention earlier that I'm one of the elders? Well, we're all very interested to see if this story of yours is true."

"I have no reason to lie." I crinkled my nose at the smoke. It had an odd smell to it. "What is this smoke?"

"This?" Foa motioned to another of the elders. "I'll let Lan explain that, since he'll be questioning you from this point forward."

"Oh. Um, alright." I'd smelled various smoke scents in my time, of course, but this one was definitely odd. Something about it just felt off. I turned to the man Foa had indicated and stared in shock as the man stood up.

The man was fairly tall, though not nearly as tall as Jun. Though of an advanced age, he didn't appear to be older than Foa; perhaps the complete lack of hair on his head hid his true age. But, for as wizened as his appearance might or might not have been, the most remarkable thing about the man before me were his outstretched hands. The smoke from the room was somehow drifting casually out of his palms. He wasn't on fire that I could tell; instead, the thin smoke simply rolled to life from his open hands, and crawled its way into the room with ease.

The man, Lan, cleared his throat and removed a small vial from a cord similar to the one that Foa wore around his chest. "Indeed, visitor. My name is Lan, and I am the elder of truth for our village. In a moment, we'll begin."

"Um, ok." Confused, I watched as Lan uncorked the vial and poured the contents into his hands. The man rubbed his hands together vigorously while muttering something under his breath, and, to my amazement, the smoke around me flashed once before taking on a more whitish hue. "What the... did you do that?"

Lan nodded, a small smile crossing his face. "Yes. But the questions are for you, not for us."

"Oh."

"First question. What is your name?"

"Mark."

The man looked past me to the smoke, and nodded after a moment. "Now, tell me your name again, but say your name is Aln."

"Um, alright." I raised an eyebrow. "My name is, uh, Aln?"

The result was immediate. The smoke around me darkened to almost pitch black, and a roll of thunder rumbled through the hut. The smoke quickly turned back to its original coloration as I gaped in wonder.

"The cantrip is active."

"The what?" I turned back to Lan. "And what was that?"

Lan held his hands up a bit higher, letting the smoke roll off his hands and across the floor. "I told you, I'm the elder of truth. Speak honest, or we will know."

I sighed. "This makes no sense."

"No sense? Alchemists are fairly common in most towns, and the largest cities would draw the more elusive evokers. Even the smallest of towns would be lax to not have at least a healer in their midst. Certainly they'd use magic in your village, what'd you call it?"

"The Undercity. And I don't have any idea what you mean by 'magic.' But if you mean the smoke and the thunder, no, no one that I've ever known could do something like that. No healer, or evoker, whatever those are."

"No one?" Lan wasn't looking at me, I realized. He was watching the clouds around us, gauging the accuracy of my responses from how the smoke reacted. Since it wasn't reacting at all, he seemed satisfied with my answers. "Interesting. You have no experience with magic?"

"I don't think so." I shrugged. "Machines and tools yes, magic, no."

"State again who you are, where you come from, and how you get there and here." Lan paused, then added, "Please."

I sighed heavily. "I'm a Pipe Worker from the Undercity. My home is called Earth. Though I've never seen it, we have one sun, not the three you have here. And when I go to sleep there, I wake up here. When I go to sleep here, I wake up there. That's as much as I know." I smirked. "Oh, and your trees don't taste very good."

"Elders?" Lan turned to the other cloaked figures and snapped his fingers. The smoke thinned immediately. "You've seen the answers. The man does not lie."

A feminine voice spoke up. "But that's impossible! To travel between worlds like that would practically require magic, and to claim he doesn't know anything at all about it? It's..."

Foa interrupted her. "It's the truth. Lan's cantrip is infallible, you all know this." He coughed once and smirked in Lan's direction. "But could you please do something about the smell of that stuff? It's horrid."

Lan shrugged. "I've tried. Can't do a thing about it." There was a quiet rumble of thunder from the smoke, and Lan glared at it. "Oh, hush you."

"Oh dear." Foa sounded amused. "Well, that is a matter for another day." He turned his attention back to me and smiled warmly. "The suns have set, and perhaps now would be a good time to test your slumber, Mark. Can you sleep with people watching you?"

I shrugged. "I'm a Worker. Not much can bother me." I looked around. "Any particular place you want me to sleep?"

Foa motioned to a section of the room. "We have set up bedding over there. You should be comfortable."

I stood and walked over to where the man had indicated, but did not see any slab or section of floor. Instead, a rectangular box had been constructed that was filled with some substance I didn't recognize. Six or seven blankets were draped across it, along with some other items I had no way of identifying. I motioned at the object. "That? You want me to sleep on that?"

"Um, is that not something you sleep on back home?"

I shook my head. "No. Workers sleep on a slab. I don't know what it's made of, but I've enjoyed sleeping on the ground here more than my slab back home. I would never be able to fall asleep on that. Here." I removed a single blanket from the contraption before me and arranged myself on the floor. The blanket was considerably thicker than anything I'd ever held and I would be warmer than I'd ever been, but it would have to do.

There was some murmuring from the elders that I ignored as I closed my eyes and began to fall asleep. Just as I was about to cross the threshold into slumber, I heard Foa call my name. I forced myself awake and said, "Yes?"

"What did you say would happen when you awaken?"

"Basically, it goes like this." I sat up on one elbow and looked at Foa. "I don't really understand it, but it's like time's not passing in either place when I'm not there. It is, but it isn't. I mean... ugh. I can't explain it. But basically, when I go to sleep tonight, I will vanish here."

"I will wake up in my home tomorrow morning. I will go about my work day tomorrow like nothing's happened. When I go to sleep tomorrow night, I'm almost positive I'll vanish from there and wake up here... and it will then be your tomorrow morning."

Foa considered this information for a moment. "So in a way, you're experiencing the same day twice, in two separate worlds, by switching in your sleep?"

I shrugged. "That's what Cerridwen thought. I don't really know."

"And Cerridwen is...?"

"Someone I'll tell you about when I'm more ready to do so."

"Fair enough. Sleep well, Mark."

CHAPTER TWENTY-ONE – WHISPERS OF REVOLUTION

I was right, that blanket was exceedingly warm. Considerably warmer than I was used to, but that only lasted for a short while. Soon enough, I cooled off and my body adjusted to a more normal sleeping temperature.

Almost immediately, I felt a hand on my shoulder and a voice near me saying my name. I jerked awake and sat up, knocking the man's hand away as I did so. It took me a moment to realize where I was, but indeed, I was back home.

Once clarity had returned, I realized Allen had awakened me. I focused on him and yawned. I had no idea how long we actually had left before the official wake up time, but that mattered little anymore. I was getting nearly twice the sleep between the two worlds as it was, so losing a bit of sleep here would matter little. "What... what are you doing here?"

"Forgot already?" He smiled. "You wanted me to see if you vanished at night, remember?" He jerked a hand toward the door. "You were right, no alarms sounded when I entered, so no one cares if we enter each other's homes."

"Oh, right." I recalled asking him to see if I disappeared when I went to sleep. Cerridwen had confirmed I did so in her world, so now I had confirmation I did it on both sides. What I was going to do with that information was an entirely different question. "So, I do, I suppose?"

"Sure do. Fascinating." Allen's eyes were shining. "So is this world of your's really that different from ours?"

"In ways I can't even begin to describe. It nearly killed me this trip." I shook my head and stood up.

"Killed you? How?"

"I nearly choked to death on the food."

"On the food? Come on. You don't choke on food."

"Keep thinking that." Grimacing, I watched as my food paste arrived for the morning. I didn't know, nor care, if Allen had had his yet for the day. The smell of the stew in the other world still lingered in my nose, and though I'd nearly died trying to swallow it, what little I'd managed to taste was beyond anything I could describe.

This grey paste, by comparison, was as tasty as eating the dirt outside my hovel. But I had no choice. This was my only meal until tonight, so it was eat it or go hungry. I hurriedly wolfed it down and sighed. "So... now what? I don't imagine you woke me up right before it was time to head to work, did you?"

"No, we have quite a bit of time." Allen yawned. "Going to be a really long day because of it."

I glared at him. "And you couldn't let me sleep longer?"

"No, I woke you up the minute you appeared. I wasn't sure if you were still alive or not."

... huh. Well, that was comforting at least. I shook those thoughts out of my head. "I was asleep, not dead."

"Any idea how you do that?"

"If I knew that, I wouldn't come back."

Allen blinked. "Really?"

There was finality in my voice when I responded with, "Yes." I'd made my mind up. That other world, with all its strangeness and oddities, even being so vastly different from my own... was also so warm, inviting, calm, and relaxing. So far, no one there had asked me to do any sort of work whatsoever, the people had seemed happy to see me, and even Cerridwen had welcomed me readily enough.

My home was dismal. Colorless. An utter void of despair and lone-liness that I and my fellow Workers were born into, slaved away within, and would die inside like many before us. The cycle would continue forever, or it would unless someone like Allen showed up.

"Wow. Quite an admission, coming from a Worker." Allen nodded at me with respect and stood up. He glanced up at the ceiling and cleared his throat. "Request."

A robotic voice queried, "Request?"

That took me by surprise. Were Workers supposed to be able to do things like that in other Worker houses? Of course, we weren't sup-posed to be in each other's houses in the first place, so maybe it was a moot point.

Allen continued, "Breakfast."

A pause, then "Granted." Allen sat down to eat his sludge as I watched. Allen caught my gaze and shrugged. "In the City above, it didn't matter where you were, you could always request anything you wanted from anywhere you were, at any time. As long as you had the credits to afford what you wanted, you got it."

"Well, that's convenient." And it sounded familiar, but I didn't know from where. I could remember, somehow, deeply imbedded in a long-forgotten memory, doing just that. Try as I might, though, the memory swam away again into oblivion as I tried to focus on it, and it was gone. I sighed and leaned up against a wall to watch Allen eat. It didn't take long; meals for Workers were enough to keep us alive, nev-er anything more. I looked up at the ceiling, trying to picture what the City above even looked like. My voice low, I asked tentatively, "Do... do you miss it?"

"What, the City?" Allen shrugged. "Sort of. It's way, way too crowded, everyone's always in too much of a hurry to get somewhere that they don't even want to be. No one's ever in much of a good mood, and it seems like it's always raining for some reason. I mean, yeah, I miss it some, because it's sure better than here."

"That doesn't really sound all that much better from here."

"You have to understand, Mark." Allen grimaced and pushed the rest of his food away. "God, that's hard to stomach still. But up there... even if you're having an absolutely rotten day, it's still your day. You have the choice to change it. If you want to hop a sky cab and fly out to the atmosphere and watch the sun set on the horizon to cheer yourself up, you can. There's a million and one things you can do from any given location and no one can tell you no. Down here, you can't even breathe without permission. And that's not right."

"I don't even know what a sky cab is." I shook my head. "How do you hop it?"

"It's like the bus, but it's not late, and you pay for it. It takes you anywhere you want it to take you."

I sighed. "I'd need a million and one people to tell me the million and one things I'd need to do on a daily basis."

Allen smiled. "You'd get the hang of it fast, I promise."

"So you say. So, how do we go about getting more people along with this plan of yours?" It still didn't sound pleasant, but I suppose by comparison, anything had to be better than the Undercity.

"We talk to them." Allen stood and moved over to the doorway. "We have plenty of time on the bus, and I'll start visiting people after the shift is over."

"You'll have to be careful of Enforcers. They have authorization to use lethal force on any Worker seen out of their quarters during non-regular hours." The words were out of my mouth before I was even aware I was speaking them.

"Pfft." Allen waved my warning off. "That's just brainwashing. I walked over here last night just fine. I doubt an Enforcer's been in this area of the Undercity in a decade, at least. They know you Workers are nothing to fear."

Allen's eyes took a dangerous glint as he stepped out the door and tossed over his shoulder, "For now, anyway!"

CHAPTER TWENTY-TWO – LIGHTING THE MATCH

I could not remember a time when anyone spoke at the bus stop. Our normal routine was simple. We showed up with about five to ten minutes to spare before the bus arrived. The bus would then be late, typically anywhere from fifteen minutes to over an hour. We stood in sullen silence, no matter the weather, waiting until it arrived, at which point we would shuffle past the soulless husks that moved past us. We'd repeat the process at the end of the day, and every day until death.

Today?

Today it was cold. There was no rain. There was no light from above, not that there ever was. No sunlight could penetrate this far into the Undercity. Only the lights from the guide lamps along the sides of the buildings illuminated the waiting area.

And today... there was no silence.

Today, you couldn't even hear yourself think. I had initially been wary of the possibility that I would have to talk to some of the other Workers myself. Besides Joe and Allen, I really hadn't talked to anyone much over the years. It just wasn't something any of us did.

My worry was for nothing. Allen had absolutely no problem talking to anyone and everyone that was willing to listen, and everyone in earshot seemed quite willing, indeed, to listen. He spoke to them at length about oppression, inequality, about how the Corporation thought nothing of them, and how they did not deserve to be treated like this.

Most of them were, as I was at first, quite wary of his words. But slowly, one by one, the lights flickered to life, long snuffed in the dark recesses of their souls. All of us were Workers, yes. We had been born, bred, and raised to be nothing more than Workers, to do a job for the Corporation. We worked day in and day out, without complaint, without fail, until our bodies gave out and we passed away.

We gained nothing from this. And we were all finally realizing this fact. As the bus rolled to a stop and we filed into our seats, the conversation continued. The entire trip, Workers did what they had never in their entire lives done before.

They turned to each other, learned the names of their neighbors, and conversed.

I learned that, to a man, not one of us was happy living in the Undercity. This place was a horrible prison of a home, and given the choice every single one of us would choose death over staying here.

I learned that a few of the Workers were banished Criminals from the City, same as Allen, though they hadn't been quite as... what was the word... charismatic? They had simply fallen in line as a Worker and become one of us. Allen had not.

I'm not sure why he was different.

As the bus approached our work detail for the day, Allen reminded us that we could not discuss any of this on the job site. We agreed, knowing that to do so would likely wind up with all of us being deprogrammed by the Enforcers. We filed off the bus to get yelled at by the Boss, only to be met not with yelling, but being told to head over to the tool benches and get ready for work.

Once again, not a word from the Boss about being late. That was something I could definitely get used to. It took a sheer force of effort for some of us, but no one mentioned anything about Allen's conversation with the Workers during the work day. More than once, though, Workers shared a lingering sidelong glance with each other.

The day's job was brutal, so there honestly wasn't much opportunity to discuss things either. The Pipe we were working on started out as a simple repair, but an hour in, the structural integrity failed and the

Pipe nearly sheared off and fell into the lava beds below. It took hours of feverish welding to reattach it with support lines just to keep it stable enough for the next team to come behind us and start the actual repair.

Exhausted, we filed into the bus after our shift was over, and I expected a mute trip home as usual. But the other Workers surprised me. Not a few minutes into the trip, they were already talking to Allen again. He was, of course, more than amiable to discuss his ideas, and it wasn't long before the entire bus was behind his plan.

So now we had the entire team ready to just stop working once we had decided it was the right time to do so. But that brought up another problem. When, exactly, was the right time to do that? How would we know? And how would we let the other Workers in on this plan?

I rubbed at my temples as the questions flew around me. I cleared my throat and conversation died. All eyes turned to me, and I grimaced. "Well, one thing you could do, if you were so inclined. Allen and I proved that there's no security on the doors like they told us. There's nothing stopping you from going door to door, seeing who is home and who isn't, and telling the Workers that way."

"There isn't?"

"Nope." I waved my hand dismissively. "I waited for the bus for like an hour too early yesterday, and Allen actually came into my hovel this morning to discuss this with me. He even ordered his meal from my house, so they also lied about that."

"You can do that?" The incredulity in the Worker's voice probably matched my look this morning.

"Yes." Allen pointed upward. "In the City proper, you can order what you want, how you want, when you want, and where you want. You're not restricted to just your own place like that. It's insane the stuff they've stuffed into your heads down here."

"So yeah." I crossed my arms and leaned against the bus seat, my head bouncing in time with the bumps in the road. "Just visit whomever is home, and the only ones you'll miss are the current working team. Have someone meet them before shift, and everyone's covered then."

One of the workers motioned at me. "You're going to do it too, right?"

"Mark?" Allen glanced at me and shook his head. "Ah, no. No, he's got... something else he's doing for me." He nodded in my direction and the Workers, satisfied with Allen's answer, continued talking amongst themselves.

I breathed a sigh of relief. No Worker could lie very well. We didn't know how. We had had that hammered into us forever. So they trusted what he said implicitly.

But Allen wasn't a Worker, not really, and he had lied. He knew that I was going to sleep to go to the other world. That I was going to leave this whole rebellion thing to his more capable hands. He had come from the main City and was able to lie.

So... could this whole thing he promised be a lie, too? That was a very sobering, troubling thought, I mused, as I watched the other Workers talk about freedom and rebellion around me.

CHAPTER TWENTY-THREE – TO EXIST OR LIVE

I was warm again. Very warm. It was odd, my home was never this... comfortable. The Corporation tended to keep things at a just tolerable level of near-frigid, and usually the only warmth was near the lava sections. So where...?

Ah. Yes. As I woke, the heavy blanket pressed on me. I must be back to... uh... whatever this place was called. It occurred to me that I really didn't have a name for this world, its people, or anything. I made a mental note that I'd have to ask someone today as I yawned, starting to wake up.

A voice nearby said, "Ah, good. You have awoken."

I looked up from the floor and nodded in greeting at Foa. "Getting there." I sat up and yawned again. "That blanket is something I think I could get used to."

"It's yours if you want it, my boy." Foa waited for me to stand before he continued, "So, we all watched you vanish last night. Strange as it might have seemed to us, the truth elder was correct; none of what you told us had been in deceit. So. You truly do come from another world?"

"I do." I shrugged. "It is what it is. I have no idea why or how this works, but there you go." I looked around. Besides Foa and myself, the building was deserted. "Where is everyone?"

"Most of the village is already up and moving around, starting their day. When I saw you appear, I set one of the children to have your meal prepared. And this time," he said with a twinkle in his eye, "I'm going to help you eat it. Give you a few pointers."

"That... would be helpful, yes." My stomach chose that moment to remind me that I'd passed on quite a lot of food yesterday and let out an audible growl of protest.

Once the food arrived, Foa spent some time explaining the nuances of eating these foods to me. I learned which foods paired best with a few varied sauces on my tray. I learned of something called seasoning, which was used to make food taste better. I learned the proper way to hold the utensils brought to me to eat with, as well as how to use them to cut the food into smaller pieces I wouldn't choke on.

And the taste of the food... The smell was heavenly, and the taste was unlike anything I'd ever imagined. Once I'd gotten over simply staring in awe at my tray, I began to work on it with gusto.

I soon discovered that a lifetime of eating the standard faire of a Worker didn't leave me much of an appetite for real food and soon enough I had to reluctantly push it away. My stomach protested the sudden influx of unknown substances and started to hurt quite savagely.

Foa stood and offered his hand to me, which I accepted. "You did much better that time, my boy. It still strikes me as strange that you've never eaten anything like this in your home, but it's obvious you tell the truth from the way you attacked your plate."

"I'll save you a step. As a Worker, if we're caught lying, we're beaten and subjected to mind wipes. After a time or two of that, you just sorta lose the desire to even try to lie." I used Foa's arm as leverage to fully stand and stretch again. "The Corporation doesn't want there to be any doubt when they ask us any questions. It's just not worth it."

Foa shuddered. "Whomever this Corporation is, they sound horrid."

"I've begun to realize that they really are." I stepped out into the world with Foa, expecting to be blinded by the light of the three suns. But today the light was rather not unlike my home, truth be told. The skies were heavily overcast, with a thick grey cloud cover obscuring every bit of sky I could see. People were, as Foa had mentioned, already going about their daily business, though a few looked our way and waved greetings.

I grimaced as my stomach turned again. "I'm... not sure I can tolerate your food. This hurts."

"I was afraid of that. Here, hold on a moment, my boy." Foa opened something on his belt and pulled a small glass object out, handing it to me. "Here, drink this. It should settle your stomach somewhat."

I looked at the object with curiosity. "Um." I didn't really have the faintest idea what, exactly, he wanted me to do with this. The shape of it wasn't familiar to me at all. "How do you open it?"

Foa laughed. "Right. I forgot." He took the object back and removed a piece of it. "Put this to your lips and drink all of it. It's got a foul taste, but it works, trust me."

I did as he asked, and he was right. It had a coppery taste, like rust mixed with blood. But a quick swallow and it was gone, and almost immediately I my stomach settled. I breathed a sigh of relief and spat to the side in a vain attempt to clear the taste from my mouth. "You were right. Foul in taste, but it seems to have worked."

"That's a little concoction I can whip up for you whenever you need it if you'd like, at least until you get used to our food." Foa accepted the bottle from me and placed it back somewhere on his belt. "Not only am I an elder of the town, I'm also one of the village apothecaries."

"Apotha who?"

"Medicine man?" Foa raised an eyebrow when I fixed him with a blank look. "Hmm. Remember the elder with the smoke?" At my nod, he continued, "Some of us don't make smoke that can tell the truth, we make you feel better instead. So, when you don't feel right, come see me. I should be able to fix you right up."

"Doctor."

"Sure. Let's go with that." As we walked, Foa pointed out a few items of interest to me. He informed me that the various plants around the houses and outside of town were, indeed, put there by the villagers. The taller grasses were something called wheat, the more odd-looking ones were called corn, and the ones that were much smaller than those two had a multitude of various names I didn't catch.

As we passed by villagers, some of them came to greet us. All knew Foa, of course, but all were also genuinely interested in greeting me, at least in passing. I was the talk of the town, both because I was new and word of my disappearance in my sleep had spread fast. But they did seem to somehow understand that I was nervous talking to people, and gave me my space. A few questions, a nod of thanks, and they would be on their way.

The chance to speak was... nice. Something I could very easily get used to.

In the center of town was a large stone well. The villagers had taken a considerable amount of time over the years to carve the stones into patterned designs to craft a very intricate display around their source of water, and the sight of it actually took my breath away. To know that someone would take their time to do something like that, simply to make something look good... And that's when it hit me.

That was the difference between my world and theirs. I looked around at the villagers and their town. That was the difference. They did not simply exist, with no purpose but the job, like a Worker did. They were not born, nameless and useless beyond a single purpose. They were born to a name, they chose their purpose, they laughed, they sang, they danced and cried.

They did not exist. They lived. Each and every one of these villagers walked around their daily lives exactly as they chose to, living as they saw fit. They had responsibilities, but even those came with choices. I understood what Allen was talking about now, fully understood it.

"Mark?" Foa snapped his fingers. "Anyone in there?"

"Hmm?" I coughed, clearing my thoughts. "I... I'm sorry. I was thinking."

"That much is obvious." Foa chuckled. "I get the feeling it's not something you've done much of prior to this."

"No, no, it's not. I've just... come to realize something about my home that's going to change here soon, and seeing your home has helped me to realize it."

"Oh?" Foa smiled. "It's a good thing, I hope."

"Well, yes, and no."

"How so?"

"I can't explain. Mostly because I'm not really sure I know." I shook my head. "Regardless, it's not your problem. What were you asking me?"

"I was asking if you wanted to go see where we were building the stables for the centidragons." Foa pointed toward the far end of the village. "Iri said she expects the eggs to hatch any time today, and you didn't get much chance to interact with either of the two beasts we have up close yesterday, so..."

"Iri? Yes, let's go there."

Foa's eyes twinkled. "I thought you might say that."

"Really? Why?"

"Give it more time, my boy, and I'll explain that one to you, too. Now come on, walk beside this old man. But not too fast... these old joints don't work like they used to."

"Old joints?" I blinked. "It was all Jun and I could to do keep up with you coming back from the forest."

"You don't understand sarcasm, do you, boy?"

"What's sarcasm?"

"Never mind. Just follow me."

CHAPTER TWENTY-FOUR –
CENTIDRAGONS

Up close, the centidragon was an impressive creature to behold. The beast was covered with interlocking scales like Cerridwen, but whereas the dragon's scales had been hard as iron and unforgiving, the centidragon's scales were rather soft and pliable to the touch. Thick rivulets of muscles rippled down the eight legs of the creature and sharp claws adorned their feet. Though it was obviously a strong beast, I found it hard to believe that the creature currently cooing and clicking contentedly as it nuzzled into my hand was in any fashion dangerous.

Jun smiled. "I think she likes you, Mark. She's never taken that quick to anyone. You've got the touch."

"I..." I was feeling emotions I did not have words for. The creature continued to nuzzle the grasses in my hand as I reached my other hand around to scratch it behind its skull, just below where its ears were attached. The reaction was immediate. The cooing intensified, and she pushed against my hand eagerly, not wanting the sensation to stop.

"Yup. You've got the touch." Jun started walking back to the holding pen where the other centidragon was eagerly watching, waiting for its turn to come meet the new person. "Want to see if you can handle two of them at once? Trial by fire kind of thing?"

"Jun! Don't you dare!" Iri popped up from behind some fencing and glared at her brother. "Mithor's way too vigorous for Mark, you know that. He gets far too excited and runs people over, and Mark's only just started working with centis!"

"Oh, I wasn't going to do it, relax." Jun ambled over to his sister and ruffled her hair before leaning up against the railing. "Besides, look at

Katha there. Man's got her wrapped around his little pinky. He's got a gift, a good one."

"Looks that way. Good thing he came here, then, because we'll need him." Iri held up a tiny piece of shell. "Guess what's starting."

Jun's eyes widened. "They're hatching?"

"One cracked just a minute ago. This piece fell off but there's still a long way to go. So yes, they are."

"Mark!"

I turned, the urgency and excitement in Jun's voice finally pulling me out of my trance with the centidragon. "Yes?"

"Want to see the centidragons hatch?"

I stood stock still for what felt like an eternity, even though the centidragon kept pushing at my hand. "H... hatch?" I remembered what Cerridwen had mentioned about her eggs, and my feet were moving of their own accord by that point. Within a few steps, I was at the fence near Iri and Jun, a bit out of breath from running.

"Oh, look out!" Iri giggled and pulled me over the fence as the sounds of eight feet eager to follow the human and his scritches happened behind me. Katha, the centidragon, stopped a foot past where I'd been standing and looked around, appearing very dejected. Or as dejected as a centidragon could appear to be, anyway.

Iri helped me stand back up on the other side of the fence, laughing. "You've gotta be careful around centis. They get overly excited and they don't stop very well for having all those legs. They don't mean anything by it, but you have to watch."

"I'll remember that."

Jun had hopped over the fence as well when the centidragon had come charging, and now he reached across it and gave the creature some scratches of affection. "We're still learning a lot about centis. These two were wild not six months ago. We caught 'em with some sleeping draught Foa whipped up, and in less than a month they were as docile as can be."

Not all of the words he said made sense to me, but I at least got the general gist of things. "What do you mean, they were 'wild'?"

"Still out there, running around in the forests and mountains and not here." Jun opened a latch on the fence, allowing the centidragon to enter the penned-in section where we were all standing. It chirped at him and dutifully stomped right on in. "Hardest part that first month is keeping them from eating their way out. Once they get the taste for eating what we feed them, though, they stop eating just anything and everything and wait for us to give them their food. Well, most of the time, anyway."

Iri smiled. "Mithor, the male, he's a chewer. He doesn't necessarily eat everything in his pen, but he's destroyed a couple of his gates already. He really likes chewing the wood."

I thought of that drink Foa had given me to settle my stomach this morning. I pointed back in the direction of his hut. "Ask Foa for something to put on it that would make it taste horrible. I bet Mithor'd stop chewing it then."

Iri turned and looked at Jun. "That... that's a great idea, Mark!"

Jun nodded. "Yep, I think we've found your calling, my friend."

My calling. Jun and Iri continued to talk as I lapsed into silence, deep in thought. My calling had always been just one thing. Swinging a wrench at a Pipe. You didn't switch jobs, it just didn't happen.

But Allen was already making things like that happen. Things back home with the other Workers were changing. I wasn't sure what I was going to wake up to tomorrow, or the next day, or the next.

If I even woke up. That was a sobering thought. If the Enforcers decided to come while we were sleeping, they'd find us easy targets. I doubted we'd even wake up if our neighbors were getting slaughtered ten feet away from where we slept. We were that well programmed.

I just couldn't see...

"Oh! Mark! Come see!" The wonder in Iri's voice was palpable, and broke me out of my reverie. It took me a moment to clear my thoughts as I focused on the other end of the penned-in section. Jun and Iri were kneeling down beside the centidragon, whom had curled up on the ground and was cooing softly at something near her stomach.

I moved over to where I could see, and the centidragon looked up at me with soft eyes. She was curled up around a hole she had dug into the ground and surrounded by debris she'd obviously stolen from around the village. A few cups, a tool or two, and various other sundries decorated the nest randomly. Mixed amongst the decorations were a dozen round items I'd come to know as eggs.

They were all moving and jerking about, cracking the shells more and more with each movement. One of the shells had already cracked enough to where a foot was sticking out, flailing about wildly as the occupant inside tried in vain to get out.

I reached down out of an instinct I didn't know I had, carefully picking up the egg with the cup of my hand. It was a big thing, filling my hand easily and quite warm to the touch. It had the same leathery feel as the centidragons themselves, and I felt the creature inside writhing and wiggling as it tried to free itself.

With wonder, I began to pick at the shell nearest the freed leg, peeling more of the shell away easily. Within a few minutes, a miniature version of a centidragon was sitting in my hand, with the only bits of shell remaining still on the creature stuck on its head.

I smiled, the first warm and genuine smile I could remember in quite some time, and said quietly, "Here, little one, let me help you with that." With my free hand, I gently removed the shell off the baby centidragon's head.

The centidragon blinked once and turned its eyes toward me. Those eyes were filled with something I'd never experienced before. I don't know what the emotions were that I suddenly found myself filled with...

But I understood them. And I knew.

I would do anything to protect this little creature in my hands. I would do anything to help give this thing a better life, to train it, to learn what I could about it.

This is what I wanted to do.

The rest of the afternoon was spent watching life begin. The remainder of the eggs all hatched, one by one, until there was a pile of broken and discarded shells to one side and a mass of wriggling, excited life on the other.

Iri asked me to move the shells away from the mother after we caught Katha twice trying to eat the discarded shells. Foa had asked her to save the shells, as components for his alchemical processes. With Katha being quite insistent on eating them, Jun gathered the remaining shells and carried them off for safe keeping.

I have no idea how long I sat there, playing with these creatures on their first day of life. It was Iri who finally, laughing, pulled me off of the pile of centidragons and pointed out that it was getting dark, and I needed to sleep soon. I only reluctantly returned to the main hut where Foa was already waiting for me with a few of the other village elders.

I was not looking forward to sleep. I did not want this day to end. Today had been unlike anything I'd ever experienced in my life by far, and ending it just didn't seem fair. It was only Foa's reassurance that I'd return on my next sleep that convinced me to pull the blanket over me and allow sleep to approach.

I would not forgive Foa if he was wrong.

CHAPTER TWENTY-FIVE - IONIZERS

I awoke on my slab with a grimace to the claxon of the wake alarm. This was most definitely not where I wanted to be anymore. But how exactly was I supposed to choose one or the other?

It was too early to try any deep thinking, and as a Worker, deep thinking wasn't really my specialty anyway. I was alone this morning, so either Allen got caught, was still too busy telling others, or was waking up himself. It mattered little. I had to get ready. My meal landed on the table in front of me, and my stomach rumbled.

After eating a few good meals yesterday in the other land, the thought of eating food paste was about as appetizing as taking a flying leap into the lava, so I left it alone. I stepped out of my home and headed to the bus stop. As I expected, Allen was already there, and he looked tired as I closed the distance to him.

He nodded by way of greeting as I approached. "Mark."

"Allen. How'd it go?"

"Thousands of times better than I could have hoped. Everyone I talked to was on board. All you Workers have been absolutely downtrodden for far too long. Time for a change, I think."

"Anyone you missed?"

"Only the last group. The ones that get off the bus when we get on, but some of the other Workers were going to talk to them. They were going to let me know if they agreed at the exchange."

I glanced up as the other Workers began to file into place. "Well, it shouldn't be too long. Based on the bus anyway."

Once the other Workers arrived, the buzz began. Their stories echoed Allen's. Every Worker they'd spoken to had agreed to help one hundred percent. To a man, we all were sick of the conditions, sick of the work, sick of every aspect of living this way. We all were willing to stop working, and see what we could do to force a change.

This was going to happen. The only possible holdouts were coming on the bus that was just now sputtering to a stop in front of us. As the door opened and the Workers on board started to file out, one of the Workers glanced at Allen and nodded.

In a gruff voice, he said, "We talked. We are all in."

"Good." Allen nodded and watched him walk away, catching my eye as he did so. There was a triumphant gleam in his eyes. He'd done it. Every Worker was ready to go. Step one was complete. Now, it was on to Step two.

But first, today we worked. The Pipe from yesterday still required major renovation and repair, and when we arrived, the bus was forced to release us in a location slightly away from the normal drop site. Heavy machinery had been brought in from another location to drill a better support column for the Pipe, and it was blocking the road.

As the crane hoisted Workers into the air to move us into position, I studied the machines carefully. They were heavy ionizers, designed to vaporize large amounts of thick materials instantly. Twenty of them were already present, twenty dirty, grimy, well-used and fantastic tools for digging.

They were even better tools to protect the Workers if Enforcers wanted to stop us from rebelling.

I made a mental note to bring this to Allen's attention on the ride home. The work today was hard, but not quite as grueling as yesterday's work had been. We were, after all, going to be replacing this Pipe eventually anyway.

As we worked, I kept glancing back over to the heavy ionizers. There wasn't a single guard to be seen protecting them. The Enforcers on site had grown lax over the years, knowing the Workers were the very definition of complacency. None of us were going to touch them unless we were told to do so. Normally, anyway.

By the end of the work cycle, another two machines had been brought in. There was no danger they'd move them in the next few days. If the Workers rebelled in the next cycle or two, we'd have the advantage of the ionizers for support.

Finally, the day was done, and we waited for the bus to finish unloading its passengers before we could board. A few of the departing Workers caught our eyes. A quick glance, nothing more... but it spoke so very much.

Foundations underneath mountains would shift with the movement of a single rock. What we were preparing to do was more than a single rock. We were an entire landmass, just waiting on a single seismic shift to break along the fault line and bring the weight of the entire City crashing down.

Whether we would survive the earthquake, only time would tell.

I told Allen on the bus home about my idea with the ionizers, and he agreed that we would use them if necessary. For the time being, though, it would be enough to simply force the Bosses and the City to listen. Violence would, hopefully, be a last resort.

It was decided. It would be soon. Very, very soon.

As we filed off the bus, our eyes met with the Workers waiting to get on. A subtle nod, a single glance. Allies, one and all. Workers ready to simply stop and wait for Allen to do whatever it was he was going to do to try to make a better life for all Workers.

I hoped he knew what he was getting us into. Once the Enforcers were brought in, it could get nasty fast. But he had a compelling argument. They couldn't go after us all, it'd be far too costly to replace us in the long run. Short term, they'd have to listen to our demands.

My thoughts awash, I muttered a noncommittal goodbye to Allen as I headed back to my home for the night. They had to listen to us, didn't they? We were the lifeblood, the source of everything that ran the Undercity, without us... there was nothing.

But what if they didn't? No, no, I couldn't think about that. I had other things to worry about, to think about, and to consider. I stepped into my home, dropped my clothes into the receptacle, took my shower, got dressed again, and took a quick look at my food paste.

The thought of trying to force myself to eat that paste had no appeal at all, knowing I'd likely have a good meal waiting for me in the other world. But I'd also not eaten since the other world, and a full day's work had left me ravenous. I sighed and sat down to eat, finishing it fast so I could move on with the day. Once on my sleeping slab, I got as comfortable as I could.

"If I could just figure out a way..." I shook my head and closed my eyes, but my thoughts kept me awake just a bit longer. There wasn't a way to stay. I knew that. But what if there was a way to move between and never return...

A way to escape this life? To leave this world behind, put down the wrenches and blowtorches, and never have to ride the bus again? The true definition of a Pipe dream.

But what a dream to dream. I drifted off with that thought echoing in my mind, over and over.

CHAPTER TWENTY-SIX - FIRE

As a Worker, I was used to waking up quickly. Typically, when the alarm claxon sounded, you had about sixty seconds before your breakfast arrived, and not much time after that before it was cleaned up. If you didn't get up and get moving quickly, you'd miss your meal and be hungry for the day. It only took a few missed meals before your body became primed to spring out of bed the moment that alarm sounded.

An alarm claxon was a great way to wake up. Coming to the other world had taught me other, admittedly rather pleasant ways, to wake. Drops of rain splattering against your face from above. Winged creatures screaming at you from their perches in the trees. A not-so-great way to wake up? Pain. A searing, white-hot pain in my leg forced its way through my sleep, demanding my attention.

I jolted awake with a cry, reaching for my leg to stop the pain. The blanket I was under, the nice heavy comfortable blanket Foa had given me the night prior, had somehow caught fire. I kicked it off and rolled away from it, fully waking up at that moment as I realized what was happening around me.

The home I was in was almost fully engulfed in flame. The roof was ablaze and it was embers from that fire that had fallen down on to my blanket and woken me. I coughed, trying to clear my lungs. I didn't know this building very well; how was I going to get out? Smoke had already filled the home. The materials used for the building construction turned out to be exceedingly good burning materials. I could not see beyond a few feet in front of me.

I closed my eyes, trying to think. I had been in fiery situations before, and it wasn't in a Worker's disposition to panic. In a Pipe, there were really only two ways out. Forward and backward. A building was a bit more complex, but in reality, there had to be at least a single entrance, right? Maybe a window or two...

A hint of a cool breeze touched the left side of my face. I heard shouts from somewhere off to my left. So somewhere that way. I coughed as the first batch of smoke started to really sear my lungs, but I couldn't worry about that; my focus had to be getting out. I dropped to the floor and crawled in the direction I hoped was the way toward safety.

The air near the floor was slightly clearer. You always entered a smoke-filled Pipe the same way, from the bottom, though I did not have the luxury of my ventilation mask here. Within a minute or two of quick crawling and working around furniture and other obstacles, I found a wall I was able to follow. Following the edge of the wall led me to a door that I kicked open.

The moment the door was open, air rushed in and the flames in the ceiling roared higher. Coughing, I scrambled out of the way as the house behind me became completely engulfed in flame. Once I was a few yards away from the house, I pulled myself up and looked around in astonishment.

The noise was astonishing. A full half dozen buildings in town were on fire, and the town was awash with the sounds of people calling out for assistance and shouting out to each other. The townspeople were doing their best to put the flames out using the water from the well, one bucket at a time via bucket brigade. Other villagers rushed between buildings that were close to those on fire, doing what they could to help ensure that the flames did not spread. A general sense of panic and fear could be felt, though from what other than the fire I did not know.

I did know this. I had to help. The building I had woken in was a total loss; hopefully I had been the only person inside and Foa had made it out. Without any other options, I ran to get in line and help with the bucket brigade. It was exhausting work, but I was used to that sort of thing. In a couple of hours, the fires either burnt themselves out or were put out by the brigade.

In all, two buildings were complete losses. Four others were damaged but could be repaired. The villagers were now taking a head count, hoping to find out how many were wounded and if anyone had died. Some sobbing could be heard here and there as the rush of putting the fire gave way to exhaustion and shock, and those that had gotten wounded were getting treatment from the village healers.

Exhausted, I lay flat on the ground, staring up into the clear blue sky and its three suns, trying not to move too much as the town continued to move around me. My legs, arms, and chest were burning from exhaustion. But it was done. The embers were only smoldering by this point, and one of the villagers had told me after the head count was complete that thankfully no one had died in the attack.

I still hadn't asked anyone what they meant by 'attack.' I wasn't sure I wanted to know. Who would attack a quiet little village like this place? But at the moment, all I wanted to do was not be so tired I fell asleep, and thereby returned to my world. I wanted to make sure my friends and my centidragons were safe first.

But before I could do that, I had to be able to walk. And that was quite questionable at this moment. A shadow darkened my view of the sky, and I blinked to focus my eyes in the sudden interruption. "Hello, Foa."

"My son." Foa carefully sat down next to me. "I'm glad to see you are well. I was worried you'd woken in that inferno and, well..." He shook his head. "Yes, ah, no sense worrying about that. You made it out, and that's that."

"I did, yes. Wasn't quite what I was expecting to wake up to." I shook my head. "What... what happened here?"

Foa shrugged. "This is what happens when you annoy a dragon. We're not sure what we did, but..."

"Wait." Exhaustion forgotten, I sat up straight on that word, my blood running cold. "Dragon." Please no, it couldn't be...

"Yep. Fairly large creature too." Foa motioned to the north. "Came from that way at speed and hit the first building from really high up with its fire breath. The second attack was my hut, but I was already outside of it and you hadn't arrived yet, so it was empty. The dragon attacked a few more times before it made a really odd sound."

Foa scratched at his head idly. "If I didn't know any better, I'd swear the dragon was crying. But whatever it was doing, after it made that noise, it didn't attack again. Instead, it simply flew off, back in the direction it came."

He shook his head. "I don't know what we could have done to aggravate a dragon, but that's not something one does lightly. We were lucky. Most towns subjected to a dragon attack are quickly levelled. Not really certain why we were spared, but..."

It had to be her. But why? I had to ask. I interrupted Foa and said, "This... is going to sound really odd, but did you get a good look at her? The dragon, I mean."

"Her?" Foa raised an eyebrow. "Well, yes, most of us did. There's hardly a cloud in the sky, and it's pretty bright today. Hard to miss a dragon attacking with that kind of backdrop. Why?"

"What color were her scales?" Please don't be grey, please don't be grey...

"Hmm." Foa considered my question for a moment. "Well, I'd have to say they were kind of a grey color, like ash. Why?"

Pipes and wrenches. "Cerridwen. It has to be. Blast it."

"You've mentioned that name before. Dare I ask who it belongs to?"

"I think you've already met." I looked to the sky, searching for signs of a dragon in flight. "Cerridwen is most likely the dragon that attacked you. Before I came to your village, I spent a few days with her. She found me one of the days I woke, and we had some very long discussions about your world and my own. Cerridwen is the one that brought me near your village. She doesn't – or didn't - bear humans much ill-will that I could tell, so I don't understand why she would attack." I shook my head. "This doesn't make any sense."

"Well, if you know this dragon, then we should discuss this with the elders immediately." Foa paused, considering, his eyes on the position of the three suns. "And though we had some time, it'd be best if we talk before you sleep, I would think. She might come back, after all."

"Agreed."

CHAPTER TWENTY-SEVEN – CIRCLE THE WAGONS

There was a stunned silence as the gathered elders and villagers stared at me with a mixture of horror and mistrust. No one spoke for a very long time. Finally, one of the other elders cleared her throat.

"You. You know this dragon? By name, you know this dragon?"

"I do."

"How by the three suns do you know a dragon by name? Dragons and humans don't interact."

I crossed my arms and stared at her. "Why don't they?"

"Are you serious?"

"Yes." I coughed to one side. I still had a bit of smoke in my lungs from the morning. "Cerridwen had opportunity to eat or kill me plenty of times when she first found me. She's huge; she could have killed me at any time without any issue. Instead, she showed me things I would have never seen otherwise, and brought me to your village. I owe her nearly everything.

"I'm not from your world. I don't know how you consider dragons. But to me, Cerridwen is a friend." I considered for a moment, looking around. "Cerridwen had been attacked by humans long ago, they nearly killed her. She has every reason to hate humans, yet she did nothing to me. She should have killed me. But she didn't.

"Instead, she showed me her family. She showed me her home. And she showed me your world how she sees it. And it's... I don't know the word. But it was beyond description. I still dream of flying among those clouds." I chuckled. "You know, when I'm not waking up in different worlds."

"Be that as it may, why would she then turn around and attack the very village she released you to?" Foa began to pace, something I'd come to recognize as a habit in the man. "We certainly couldn't have done anything to anger her, have we?" He glanced at another elder. "Ian, what say you? Have any of the hunters found anything out of the ordinary on their excursions lately? Anything that might be construed as a dragon's hunting grounds that we're trespassing on?"

The elder, Ian, a grey old hawk of a man, considered the query. "None that I can think of. The strangest thing anyone's found in half a season is standing here today."

"Well, yes. But not even any dragon sign? No tracks, no prey carcasses, nothing?"

"No, nothing at all."

"So it can't be that. And you mentioned family, Mark?" At my nod, he continued, "So she would have a nest somewhere within flying distance of here, but that's a big range. I'm assuming an egg clutch that has not hatched, since she was alone and did not have any dragonlings with her?" When I nodded again, he said, "Depending on when they were laid, those eggs could take a decade to hatch, so it can't be that she's showing them to hunt. So then what..."

Another elder spoke. "We do not have the means to defend ourselves, Foa. If she comes back and decides to land, we will be slaughtered. From the air, at least the most she can do is catch our homes on fire. We can survive that, given enough warning. If she lands, we're all dead. We can't defend against an angry dragon, she'd tear us all to ribbons!"

Foa frowned, deep in thought. "Agreed. The only thing we could do then is flee. We should let everyone know that if she is sighted again, they need to head into the woods and not look back." He sighed. "If she returns, it will be to kill. We got lucky once, the next time we won't be. Maybe it'd be for the best if we abandon our homes and start over..."

"No."

There was a long silence as Foa stopped pacing and all the elders turned to look at me. Finally, Foa cleared his throat and said, "I'm sorry, but... no? You think we should stay?"

I nodded slowly. "At home, I'm about to fight for what I feel is right. It scares me to my very core, and it's something I've never done before, but it's right. The same applies here. This isn't right."

Foa cast an odd look at me. His features were stern, but there was a twinkle in his eye. "We can't fight a dragon, Mark. Even the strongest alchemists in the village are mainly skilled in healing and nature related magics. So we should just stay to get eaten?"

I crossed my arms again and frowned. "Not eaten. She told me she doesn't like the taste of man. But this... this is a misunderstanding, it has to be. I know Cerridwen. She is a good person. Dragon. Whatever. There has to be a reason she's doing this." I sighed. "I just don't have any idea what it could be."

Foa swept his walking stick in a wide arc. "Well, I doubt she's going to listen to any of us besides you. Her attack was while you were still in your world, so you could not help us. What would you have us do?"

"Let me think." I looked up at the skies, my thoughts racing. Why would she have attacked like that? This didn't make any sense. There had to be a way to send a message that the villagers meant her no harm.

I wasn't sure if a large sign would do the trick. I didn't know if the villagers could read or write, for one, and there was no assurance that Cerridwen would understand the written language of the villagers. Did dragons even have a written language? Also, for her to be able to read the sign as she was flying it'd have to be huge. So that wasn't feasible.

If I were back home, of course, there were various force shields we could erect in no time flat. Fire retardant domes, even just installing fire suppression systems around the village would mitigate the damage Cerridwen's fire breath could do. Granted, this wouldn't help if she landed and just started attacking with her claws and tail...

Wait. Land. Get her to land. If there was a way to just get her to land and wait for me to arrive from the other world, I could talk to her and find out what was going on. But how to do that...

"I have an idea." I started to pace, emulating Foa. Surprisingly, it seemed to help with the thought process. "Cerridwen isn't going to listen to any of you, so if she comes while I'm gone, you'll have to stall her until I arrive, correct?"

"I would think that is correct, yes. But how do we do that, exactly?"

"You have to show her that you are not a threat. She has to be able to see that you mean her no harm." I looked up into the sky, watching the clouds. "You need to have someone watching the sky. That's where she will come from. She will be able to see you from a very long distance away, much further than you'll see her, but you should still have plenty of warning before she arrives."

Foa glanced at me with curiosity. "How do you know this?"

"When she brought me here, I rode on Cerridwen's head."

There was a collective gasp of shock from around me. One of the elders said in a shaky voice, "You... you rode the dragon? That's impossible!"

I shrugged. "Believe what you will. Cerridwen said that was a better option than carrying me in her claws, since she didn't want to hurt me and her claws are pretty sharp. Honestly, the hardest part was figuring out how to climb up in the first place. Once I was up by her skull, it was pretty easy to hold on."

Foa examined my face carefully. "You're not lying, are you, my son?"

"I told you, Workers aren't very good at lying, so most of us don't bother. And I just don't see the point in lying, especially when it's about something this critical, now do you?"

For a minute, all the elders simply stared. Finally, one of them tentatively said, "So, ah... so one of us watches the sky, yes?"

"Yes." I nodded in affirmation. "The minute you see Cerridwen in the air, you have to do something she's not expecting. It can't be a threatening gesture, but it has to be something unusual enough that she wouldn't attack."

"Such as?"

I continued pacing, my eyes falling upon the city well. "Hah. I've got it." I pointed to the well. "There's plenty of clearance around the well for everyone in town to spread out. Have everyone converge here and lay down on the ground. Men, women, children, everyone needs to get down and stay down, an equal distance from each other starting at the well. It needs to make a pattern she can see from the sky, all around the well. That will hopefully make her curious enough to land. "I grimaced. "But then someone will have to ask her to please wait until I arrive, so we can work this out."

Foa nodded. "I will speak to her if she will allow it. But what do we do if she still attacks?"

I frowned. "Then you run. And when I arrive, I'll still try to talk to her if she's here."

Foa's voice was quiet. "Mark, she'll kill you."

"Maybe. Maybe not. You don't know that, and I don't know that. But I... I have to try. I have to know why."

CHAPTER TWENTY-EIGHT –
TROUBLE BREWING

My dreams were starting to become clearer. As before, I'd seen a family in my dreams, and this time I felt confident I knew them. They were my family. I did not know them, but I felt strongly that the parents standing in my dream, signing something, were definitely my mother and father. But too soon the dream ended and I was once again without an answer.

I woke up in a foul mood as the alarms blared. I wanted this day to end and end fast. There was too much going on in the village to be spent swinging a wrench over a broken Pipe! Which, obviously, meant the day was going to move as slow as a lava flow in a dormant volcano. But regardless, it was what it was, and I had a job to do.

I realized as I stood up that the smell of smoke still clung to me like a blanket. That wasn't much of a worry, though. Workers rarely smelled very good, even after their cleansing for the day. Working on the Pipes was a very sour, smelly job, and routinely the scent of a particular nasty job would linger for days.

My breakfast slid onto the table with a sickening flump. I sighed and decided I had better eat it today. With the fire, food in the other world had been sparing at best, and if I didn't eat the food paste often enough, someone would likely start to take notice.

Come to think of it, I still wasn't really sure how exactly the two worlds synched with each other. I frowned as I ate, trying to figure out how that worked. I woke up in each location appropriately enough. If I went to sleep in my world, when I returned to my world, it was right after the sleep cycle I'd gone to sleep in.

Which made no sense, because I had just spent easily ten to sixteen waking hours in the other world. And each day here in my world was highly regulated; sixteen hours on the job, eight hours for rest and food and travel to and from the job site. Granted, the bus was typically late, so we often got less sleep time, but no Worker ever really noticed the lack of sleep anymore. So how did sixteen hours in the new world equal less than five or six hours here?

I shook my head to clear my thoughts. Those thoughts were for someone more versed in analytical thinking than me. I was a Worker, nothing more, nothing less. Though perhaps I was now a Worker and a centidragon handler? That thought brought a new feeling bubbling to the surface, and I smiled through the bland taste of the food paste I was eating.

Happiness. Such a rare feeling in this world, and something I felt quite often in the new world. If there was just some way I could transition over and never return, I knew I wouldn't even look back for a second glance. I'd leave behind every wrench, every Pipe, and every Worker in a heartbeat. But that wasn't an option. I didn't even know how this whole thing even started, much less how it worked. So for now, I had to be content to simply live two separate lives, and see what happened.

I sighed and pushed away the remainder of the food paste, my appetite gone. The stuff was terrible. I grimaced as a noise caught my attention; the sound of water landing on what passed as a roof for my home. It was raining, again.

By the time I got out to the bus stop, the rain was coming down at a fairly good pace. It was unusual for it to rain heavily here in the Undercity, but not unheard of; occasionally a tropical storm or a flood would happen somewhere far above, and as a result we'd wind up with heavier moisture. That wasn't much of a reassurance, mind you; all it did was make a cold and wet day that much wetter.

Allen nodded as he walked up. He glanced around to ensure no one else had reached the bus stop yet before he asked, "Have a good sleep?"

I knew what he was implying, of course. I shook my head. "Not exactly. I woke up to the house on fire."

"What?"

"Between the dragon attacking, putting out the fires, and the plan we came up with in case she comes back again... it's really difficult to explain without sounding like a lunatic, so maybe I'd better tell you later, when I get a better chance to work out how to say it." I shrugged. "I really wish I could show you how I get there."

"Me too. This place sounds a lot better than here. You know, other than waking up in a fire." Allen smiled. "But we're going to make here better, and soon. You'll see. Just need to make sure a few stragglers from the prior shift are onboard, and then we're ready to go."

"Should know that when the bus arrives, right?"

Allen nodded. "Hopefully." We both lapsed into silence, the rain giving percussive music to our thoughts as we waited for the bus. It showed up remarkably on time today, thankfully granting us temporary relief from the heavy rain.

As the bus unloaded its passengers, one of them passed by Allen. He met Allen's eyes and said gruffly said, "We're in. 100%."

"Good." The simple exchange done, Allen's eyes met mine and sparkled with excitement. His plan was ready. All that was left to do now was to start the ball rolling. And with the ionizers in place as well, it had to be soon or they wouldn't be available as backup.

I felt something odd in my stomach. A kind of fluttering, weird sensation that made me want to keep shifting my feet around and fidget with things. I'd never felt this before, and I didn't know what it was.

Was it nervousness? I had never been nervous before that I was really aware of, though I suppose it could have been that. After all, there was a lot at stake. My thoughts rolling, I boarded the bus with the rest of the Workers to do our daily ride into the depths of hell.

The ride was, as usual, monotonous. The Workers chatted amongst themselves, emboldened by Allen's presence and the idea that soon they might be allowed to have personal freedoms for their very own. It was a sobering thought to realize that in such a short time, every single Worker had come around to Allen's ideas. That fast, and we were behind him as a single entity.

It bespoke how long we'd been repressed, I guess. I watched the tunnels and mines go by through the smeared window as we drove, my mind elsewhere. With centidragons and villagers to remember, fields of grasses and forests of trees to think about, and delicious meals of foods I had never tasted before to dream of, it was hard to concentrate on the here and now.

Finally, the bus slammed to a stop with a snarl of brakes, and we filed off into our assigned places. Conversation came to a halt once the bus stopped. We might be dreaming of freedoms, but it hadn't happened yet, and we were no fools. Though we had been picked up on time, our trip in had not been speedy enough and we were late. As usual, the Boss was standing in his well-worn spot with a gleeful grin plastered across his face.

That was never, ever a good sign.

We had barely gotten in our places when he started up. "Well, Workers, what have we here?" He looked directly at Allen. "Late again, and is our little City fallen angel going to yell at the big Boss again to keep you rats from getting in trouble, just like last time?"

Allen smirked. "If I have to, I will."

I had never seen the look I saw cross the Boss' face on anyone's features before, and I felt a chill in my very bones. A sneer broke across his face, and he chortled, "Oh. Oh, ho ho ho, I was so hoping you were going to say that." He raised his arm and snapped his fingers, once.

All the Workers heard the sound at the same time. A high-pitched whine of machinery, a sound that ripped across your spine like dragging a wrench the wrong way down a Pipe over and over again until you couldn't stand it anymore. As one, our heads turned to look to our left.

One voice whispered in horror what the rest of us were screaming in our heads. "Enforcer!"

CHAPTER TWENTY-NINE – ENFORCER

I had only seen an Enforcer once before, and that was officially once more than I ever cared to see them. Though we were told in what little schooling we received that Enforcers were still technically human, the robotic thing that approached us right now bore little resemblance to either the Boss or any Worker.

It easily stood over six feet tall, or it would if it had any legs remaining. From the knees down, the limbs had been replaced with a rotating disk that projected some form of anti-gravity field that allowed it to both hover and move absurdly fast if the need called for it.

The Enforcer's arms had been replaced as well. One arm was a long cylinder of some form of metal with a circular ball at the end of it. Electricity arced from the ball occasionally, striking the ground as the Enforcer moved. The other arm was a monofilament chain whip, also electrified, that crackled and snapped as it moved.

The torso, neck, and head of the Enforcer were all fully enclosed behind the same metal material that made up the arm. There were no visible eye or breathing holes. It was a terrifying vision of subjugation, of enforcement, of submission and Corporation control.

It moved in a straight line directly at Allen, ignoring everyone else. The other Workers, myself included, immediately scattered to a safe distance; no one ran far, for none of us wanted to incur Corporation wrath for fleeing the scene, but we also didn't want to be too close to the Enforcer if it decided to attack.

Allen, incredibly, stood still and simply watched the Enforcer come. He didn't move. He didn't run. He didn't even look away. The

Enforcer came within a few feet of him and hovered ominously, waiting on word from the Boss on its next instruction.

The Boss gleefully looked at Allen and asked, "So, big man, what do you think now? Think you need to yell at me? Or are you going to let me do the yelling from now on, like I'm supposed to? Huh? Huh?"

Allen raised an eyebrow. "I think you're just letting an Enforcer do your job for you. That you're as low in the Corporation chain as the Workers are, and you're terrified that they know it."

There was a moment where no one moved. No Worker blinked, Allen simply stood by, the Enforcer hovered and the Boss's face got redder and redder. Then, a single howl of fury.

The first blow fell.

Then the next. And the next.

I am ashamed to say that I turned away. I could not watch. I could hear the sickening sounds of impacts against meat, the sizzle of electricity frying open wounds, and the Boss's cackling a haunting backdrop against it all. It was horrifying, and the sounds will last in my memories for the rest of my life.

But oddly, through it all, Allen made very little noise. He cried out a time or two, yes. Anyone would have done so, it would have been impossible not to. But he never once asked for it to stop. He never cried for mercy. He never begged, never said he was wrong, nothing. He simply... took it.

Once the blows stopped, I dared look back. Allen was alive, though he lay in a crumpled heap. His skin was sizzling from the electrical impacts against bare skin. Most of his meager clothing had been flayed away, and his exposed skin was bruised or bleeding. But he was alive.

The Boss spat on him and turned to us. "Anyone else?" When no one responded, he nodded. "Good. Time for work."

We moved to our tools as one unit, what we'd just witnessed burning into minds. But, what we had seen wasn't necessarily what the Boss had wanted us to see. I glanced back over at Allen, who was still unconscious. Smoke rose from his clothing, and the Enforcer stood guard near him.

As the crane lifted me up into the air, I caught the eye of one of the other Workers near me. What I saw in his eyes surprised me. I did not see fear, as I expected. Instead, I saw something I had never seen in another Worker before.

Determination. They had hurt the de facto leader of the Workers, whether the Boss realized it or not. And without knowing it, they had energized the resistance movement by their very actions. All just by one act of bringing a single defiant Worker in line.

I understood then what Allen had just done. He had proven his point. He was alive. Even someone like him, someone new to the Undercity and completely untrained to the ways of a Worker was still too valuable to outright kill. They would have to replace him, and that cost time and resources. Both things they couldn't spare.

So they hadn't killed him. They couldn't. They could beat him, torture him within an inch of his life, try to force him to do what they wanted him to do all day long, but they couldn't kill him. By allowing them to hurt him, Allen had shown us just exactly how much power we truly had.

Everyone watching had understood that lesson implicitly. Throughout the day, as we worked on the same blasted worthless pipes, our eyes kept getting drawn back to Allen's unconscious form, far below. If the Boss noticed, I'm sure he attributed it to our being reminded of what happened if we stepped out of line. Instead, it was a beacon, a reminder of what life was like now and how it should never be, and how it would never be again.

Finally, the day was over and the crane descended, returning us to our toolboxes. As I detached, I felt a hand on my shoulder and I froze. I turned and saw the Boss directly behind me.

"You. Worker."

"Y... Yes, Boss?"

He motioned to another Worker nearby. "You, Worker!"

The other Worker snapped his head up in attention. "Yes Boss!"

"You two, go collect that Worker and carry him onto the bus. Drop him wherever, I don't care, just get him out of here." He motioned to Allen.

"Yes Boss!" We echoed. I felt a wave of relief. I didn't like being that close to the man. Ever. The other Worker and I moved to collect Allen's unconscious form, and I hesitated as we got near the Enforcer.

This close to the Enforcer, I felt the static electricity in the air pulling on the hairs on my body. I pulled on Allen's body, trying to pick him up as the other Worker grabbed him from the other side.

If the Enforcer saw me or even noticed me, it made no reaction at all. It simply ignored me entirely as the other Worker and I moved Allen's unconscious body over to the side where the bus would arrive.

Allen was not all that heavy, a fact that surprised me. Coming from the well-fed City above, I expected him to have more girth. He was bulky enough that it wound up taking two of us to move him successfully, so I was thankful that two of us had gone. As we waited, I examined his injuries as best I could without looking conspicuous. Most of his wounds looked painful but didn't look all that bad. Nothing that would explain why he'd been unconscious all day. Unless...

Ah. I felt Allen chuckle ever so slightly in my arms. So some of this was for show, for the benefit of the Boss, to make him think he'd won. Alright, I could accept that. I had to admit, Allen was a smart man.

As the bus pulled up, I heard the Boss behind us saying something to the Enforcer, but I could not hear it over the screeching of the bus's breaks. After the Workers filed out, my team filed on and the bus pulled away.

The other Worker and I carefully placed Allen in a seat, and I sat beside him to brace him as we rode. Once the work detail location was out of sight, Allen opened his eyes and stretched. "Ugh... god, that was hard to do."

The bus echoed with a chorus of cheers and shouts that he was ok, but Allen waved them off. "Yes, yes, I'm alright. But it was important that... ow. That you all saw that." He winced in pain.

Another Worker nodded. "We saw, yes. So what do we do now? We don't have to stand that like you did, do we?"

"You can if it comes to it, I promise, but let's hope it doesn't come to that." Allen coughed. "I think it's time. One Enforcer has arrived. That's one too many already. If he ever gets wind of this little project of ours, he'll call more. So we have to act, and act now."

"Tomorrow. Spread the word. Tomorrow, we act."

CHAPTER THIRTY – CERRIDWEN

I awoke carefully, fearful of more flame and fire. To my relief, there was nothing. No fire, no flame, no smoke, and no cries of villagers putting out additional fires. With the destruction of the main elder's meeting hut yesterday, I had gone to sleep in an outlying hut, and thankfully it appeared that Cerridwen had not attacked today.

As I continued to wake, it occurred to me that I wasn't hearing any noises at all. Normally, the village was bustling with various sounds all day long. People would talk, laugh, and sing. There would be sounds of wood being chopped, food being served, items being hauled by centidragons, and other noises.

I didn't even hear one of those bird things making noise. Something didn't feel right. I picked my way around the hut until I made it outside and looked around.

Every villager that lived here was currently lying prone in a pattern around the well in the center of town. They looked terrified, absolutely terrified. Sitting on the well, looking fairly calm given the situation, Foa was whittling away on a stick with a small knife.

Behind him, on the other edge of the village, Cerridwen was pacing slowly in a wide path. She had not seen me yet.

Foa glanced up as I approached, and his eyes lit up. He motioned at the dragon.

I waved a greeting to him and turned toward Cerridwen, clearing my throat. "Cerridwen, I'm here."

She stopped pacing and turned. "So you are." The dragon sat down, facing me, and waited for me join her. She studied me as I approached,

150

growling, "You are an awful brave human, to freely walk up to an angry dragon."

"I have done nothing to make you angry, Cerridwen." I stepped carefully around the villagers as I made my way over to her. It wasn't an easy task; my path to her was through quite a few villagers, and I was doing my best to not simply trip and fall over.

After a moment, Cerridwen sighed with exasperation. "Alright. Look, humans. I'm not going to attack now, alright? Those of you on the ground, you've made your point. You can stand up and move off to the side, let Mark through before he falls over, please."

I stopped long enough for the villagers to stand up and quickly scatter back to the well, where they gathered in a tight circle to watch the proceeding. Once they were out of the way, I walked over to Cerridwen easily. I looked up at her and frowned. "Why did you attack them yesterday, Cerridwen?"

"Why? Why should I not have? The only reason I'm not boiling over with anger right now is because I've had time to calm down since landing." Cerridwen's voice was tense. "I found my nest destroyed! The only reason I didn't destroy everything here in return yesterday was because I was too overcome with grief. I came today to finish the job."

I blinked. "What? Nest destroyed?"

Cerridwen moved her head down until she was face to face with me. I have to admit, it was pretty imposing. "Why did you humans attack my nest and slaughter my children?"

I took a step back. "I... I'm afraid I don't understand."

"Yes, Mark." Cerridwen's voice was sad, but tinged with anger. "Your human friends came to my nest when I was hunting, destroying every egg there. They killed my children. You had to have told them where I lived, for no one else knew of my lair. So you told them about me, and they came, and took everything. So you ask why I attacked? That is why."

"No." I shook my head. "That... that can't be." I frowned as I realized something. "Wait. No, that absolutely can't be true."

"Oh?" Cerridwen's voice held an edge to it that I wasn't sure I liked. "How, pray tell, could that absolutely not be true?"

I turned around and motioned toward the villagers. "They didn't even know that I knew you until after you'd attacked. I had told a few of them your name, yes, but not who you were or that you were a dragon. Also, I don't know where your home is, Cerridwen, beyond roughly how to reach it from air. Last time I looked, I haven't just suddenly figured out how to fly. I don't have the slightest idea how to get to your cave from the ground."

I turned back to Cerridwen. "And one more thing. I would never, ever tell anyone where you live without your permission, even if I could give them exact directions and a map straight to your cave entrance. You were the first living thing in either of the worlds I've lived in to ever show me any kindness, friendship, or trust. Why would I betray that?"

Cerridwen was silent. I heard a sound behind me, and I glanced over my shoulder to see Jun carefully approaching. He knelt down, low, and said, "M'lady, if I may?"

Cerridwen looked at him but didn't respond.

Jun continued, "I do not know where your nest is, m'lady. But all of our people are currently here in town. No one is out hunting, or exploring, or even working the fields beyond what they can reach and return from in the same day. Unless your nest is next door, it could not have possibly been one of us."

Cerridwen growled, "There's not another human settlement around for six day's flight in any direction. If not you humans, then who?"

Jun paused. "I... do not know, I'm afraid."

For a time, we simply stared at each other. Cerridwen finally looked at me. "Mark, I must know. Was it your idea?"

"My idea? Was what my idea?"

"To have the inhabitants of this village lay down in an absolutely absurd pattern that I could see from above. The moment they spotted me this morning, it was like ants in a disturbed anthill. All these little movements, all going to the center of this village. Then suddenly, they spread out and I could see a distinct pattern, even from the sky."

Cerridwen made an odd sound and thin wisps of smoke curled up from her teeth and snaked their way to the sky before dissipating. "I had never seen anything like that. So I flew in close, high enough to avoid any sort of hidden attack... but nothing, and still no one moved. I landed here, and watched, and still nothing happened. Finally, one of the villagers, the old man, came over and asked that I wait for you to arrive from your world before we did anything else. I agreed, so here we are."

"Ah. Well, yes. That basic idea was mine. I wanted to make sure you saw something that would let you know they weren't a threat, so you wouldn't attack." I turned and looked at the villagers, who were watching us intently. "They have welcomed me, as I think was your intention when you left me here. I couldn't bear the thought of you hurting them, or they hurting you. I had to stop it, and the only way to do that was to talk to you. So, well... that was what I thought would work."

Cerridwen looked at the villagers. "It did."

Another long pause followed. Finally, I said, "Cerridwen, you said your children were attacked?"

"Yes."

"Could you take me to see them?"

Cerridwen stared at me in astonishment. "Why in the world would I agree to that? You've already destroyed them once."

Jun cleared his throat. "Actually, m'lady, Mark has a point. We might be able to find out who actually slaughtered your babies with more... eyes..." He paused as Cerridwen fixed her gaze on him.

"We?"

Jun held his broad arms out wide. When he spoke, it was slow and careful. "Yes, we. I am one of the village trackers and hunters. As you can see, I carry no weapons. I have nothing on me to harm you, nor do I have any wish to harm you. But my job is tracking and identifying creatures, and I want to help you find whomever did this." He smiled ruefully. "No offense, Mark, but probably I can track them considerably better than you can."

I shrugged. "I won't argue there."

Cerridwen studied Jun for a long minute before she finally nodded. "Fine. Both of you will come. We will find who did this to my babies, or I will reconsider my distaste of human flesh. Do we have a deal?"

Jun said, "Agreed."

I sighed. Between the Enforcer in my world, and an angry dragon in this world, life just wasn't going to ever be easy, was it? "Agreed."

CHAPTER THIRTY-ONE – DISCOVERY

As long as I live, I doubt I'll ever find a sensation quite as exhilarating as dragon flight. I can't ever adequately describe it. The words I know as a Worker are woefully inadequate to explain the feelings I get as the ground drops away below us, the wind tries to peel me off of Cerridwen's back with each gust, or the sheer intensity of the views in every conceivable direction.

Behind me, I felt Jun's face pressed into my back as hard as he could shove it. For all the big man's bravado, apparently either heights were not the best for him or he simply couldn't handle dragon-back riding. Granted, he was seated lower on Cerridwen's neck than I was; perhaps the ride was rougher there? I didn't know. Regardless, though we'd been in the air for well over two hours, it wouldn't be too much longer now. I recognized the mountain range we were flying toward as the one that housed Cerridwen's cave.

Cerridwen landed with much less grace than normal outside the cave entrance and growled. "We are here. I suppose you want me to light your way into the nest?"

"No." I shook my head, though Cerridwen could not see it. "No sense in doing that. Just get us to your nest, then give us some light. Let us see what we're dealing with, and see what we can find. After that, well... whatever you wish to do, you are free to do."

Jun groaned. "I don't think I like flying."

Cerridwen's voice was low. "Human, a warning. You vomit on my neck or shoulders, and you will be cleaning it up before I throw you off the cliff side. Am I clear?"

"As a bell."

Without another word, Cerridwen ducked her head under the tunnel's entrance and started down into her nest. I cleared my throat. "Ah, Jun, I feel I should mention something."

"What's that?"

"What's the darkest place you've ever been in your life?"

Jun thought for a moment as the light dimmed around him. "Mmm, probably when I fell into a ravine a few years ago, I spent a couple of days at the bottom of it until I was found because I broke my foot, why?"

I chuckled. "You're about to experience a new breed of dark. Just trust in Cerridwen, she knows where she's going and will see us through."

"You do realize the irony in what you're saying, right?" There was a hint of amazement in Cerridwen's voice from somewhere up ahead.

"Honestly, m'lady... I don't think he does."

We walked for some time in total darkness, the only sound coming from Cerridwen's footfalls against stone. Unlike before, we did not stop to see interesting sights along the way; we had a specific goal in mind, and Cerridwen was in no mood for conversation. It was a grueling exercise in patience, and without any visual cues to know how we were progressing, it was impossible to tell how far we'd walked.

Finally, Cerridwen growled, "We have arrived," and I felt her bend down to allow us to dismount from her shoulders.

I hopped down first then said, "Jun, I forgot to mention this. You'll have to make your way down her body without any light."

"Right." There was the sound of movement, and then a thud as Jun landed somewhere off behind me. He had literally jumped off of her and collapsed on his butt.

"That was rather graceful." Cerridwen's voice was wry. "You humans never cease to amaze me."

"Most of what I hurt was my pride." Jun said as he stood up. "So, how are we to examine your nest? As Mark said, this is a whole new level of darkness."

"If you could see as I could, you could see the nest clearly." There was sadness in Cerridwen's voice. "Egg shells everywhere, my babies gone. Nothing left but emptiness and death."

I sighed. "But Cerridwen, we can't. We need some light to see, so if you could, please?"

"If I must." There was a low rumble from deep inside the dragon, and flame erupted from within her mouth, headed to the ceiling. Cerridwen pulled the flame into her mouth as before, letting the flame flicker just past her teeth as she looked at Jun and I.

"By the three suns," Jun breathed. "That's terrifying."

"Isn't it?" I smiled. I looked toward the nest now that I could see, and it was exactly as she described. It was heartbreaking. The stone eggs had been decimated, broken into pieces by some unknown source. A strange yellow substance, I assumed the contents of the eggs, was splashed all over the place, and...

"Cerridwen?" Jun moved quickly over to the nest. "These are footprints."

Cerridwen's eyes narrowed behind us, but she did not respond.

I cleared my throat. "Uh, Jun? When she's doing that to give light, she can't talk. So just talk to her and she'll respond when she can."

"Ah. Makes sense." Jun moved into the nest and poked around. He moved some shell pieces around and peered carefully into sections of the nest before he began searching in an ever-widening circle around the nest. Finally, he moved back over to Cerridwen and I and nodded, once. "Alright. M'lady, you may extinguish your flame so you may talk. I know what happened."

The flame went out immediately. "Footprints. You found footprints. How did I not find footprints?"

"Dragons are rumored to be able to see in total darkness. Given we came all the way down here without any light, I'm going to assume this is true. In the light, they are easy to see. With, let's call it, your underground vision, you could not see the footprints. They mostly likely blended in with the ground and were invisible to your other vision. In the light, I noticed a very obvious set of prints going up the wall directly beside the nest to the right. Do you see them?"

I heard movement in the darkness, then Cerridwen replied, "No. Let me check with some light." A roar of flame, and it was as Jun said. There was a set of odd-shaped footprints that went right up the wall. Whatever the footprints were, they were obviously not humanoid; they were far, far too large. The flame went back out, and all was silent again.

Finally, Cerridwen said quietly, "I... I am a fool, aren't I? I attacked you humans in haste. I killed for revenge, for my babies that had been slaughtered by hands that weren't even yours. I can never be forgiven."

"Rest easy, m'lady." Jun's voice was soothing in the darkness. "For I have two pieces of good news there."

"What possible good news could you have?" Cerridwen's voice was incredulous.

"No one was seriously hurt during your attack. I believe the one that was closest to any of the direct fire was, unfortunately, Mark himself. He woke up in one of the buildings that was engulfed in flame."

"What?" I felt Cerridwen turn toward me in the darkness. "You woke up in... oh Mark, I'm so sorry."

I shrugged, knowing she could see my reaction. "It's not my first time inside something that was on fire. I survived, so no worries."

"You say that, but it bothers me. I will make it up to you. I swear it." Cerridwen paused, then continued, "You mentioned two pieces of good news?"

"Yes." I could hear the smile on Jun's face even if I couldn't see it. "They didn't get all the eggs."

"W... what?"

"Toward the back, under a bunch of cracked eggs, two of your babies were missed. M'lady, you are still a mother."

"O.. Oh!" I heard a scratching and a scrambling of claws on stone as Cerridwen abandoned us and headed straight to her nest. I heard the sound of what I assumed was empty shells being tossed to the side unceremoniously, and then...

An odd sound. Like a purring, a very happy, contented, loving sound, a sound I'd never heard before but recognized immediately as that of a mother speaking to her children.

As Cerridwen consoled herself with her remaining eggs, I sat down on the ground to avoid tripping in the absolute darkness. "Jun, do you have any idea what might have done this?"

"Idea, no. Know for absolute certain, yes."

I sighed. "Please don't talk in riddles. I'm just a Worker, I don't do riddles."

Jun chuckled. "I'm sorry, Mark. Let's see if you can figure it out though. I've told you a few things about our world, right?"

"Well, yes."

"Do you remember me telling you about something that would eat pretty much anything, including something like a stone? Or in this case, an eggshell that's as hard as stone?"

The realization of what he was talking about hit me like a wrench against a pipe. "You're kidding."

"Nope. Those are centidragon tracks going straight up the wall. So there's a nest somewhere, and if we don't find it, they'll come back and finish the job."

Finish the job. Take away the last little bit of family that Cerridwen had in this world. "That is not going to happen."

CHAPTER THIRTY-TWO – HOPE

After Cerridwen had spent enough time with her remaining eggs, she moved back over to us and lit her flame so we could see. Now that I was looking for centidragon paw prints, I could make them out and saw Jun's point easily enough.

And they were everywhere. All through the nest, covered in what Jun called egg yolk and mud, and going all up and down the walls. But where had they come from? They weren't diggers that Jun was aware of, so it didn't make sense that they'd come this deep after Cerridwen's nest. They had to have an access point somewhere, but none of the footprints went the way we'd come into the nest.

So the question remained. How did they get here? I frowned, tracing the line of footprints up the wall and into the darkness with my finger time and time again. Too many disappeared into the darkness. That couldn't be coincidence.

"Hey, Jun. Do you mind waiting here for a minute?"

Jun shook his head. "Long as you don't leave me here permanently, I'll be fine for a few. Why?"

"I want to check something." I moved over to Cerridwen. "Can I climb up? I need to check something while you're still alight."

She nodded, but looked worried.

I smiled. "I'll be careful of the flame." After she moved down, I carefully picked my way around her head and to the spot near her neck where I could ride. "Ok, I'm on. Now, if you could, Cerridwen, follow some of those tracks up the wall there. Go slow so we can keep an eye on them. I want to see where they go."

Cerridwen answered me by moving her head along one of the foot-print path tracks. It was a bit winding; apparently the centidragon had been distracted, or they did not see in total darkness as well as full dragons But eventually the tracks disappeared into another tunnel located near the very top of Cerridwen's cavern, a much smaller tunnel that she could never have fit inside if she had tried. Many tracks emerged from this tunnel besides the one we'd followed up.

"This looks like the entrance." I closed my eyes, listening. Everything was dead silent, but against my cheek, I thought I felt the faintest hint of air. "Hmm." I opened my eyes again and examined the tunnel.

It was very similar to Cerridwen's entrance tunnel, just much smaller in scale. Most likely it was a secondary lava shunt that probably had run off the main line down a fault in the stone somewhere years ago. "It's another lava tube, smaller. I think I feel air coming down it. Best bet, it goes to the surface."

The light winked out as Cerridwen spoke. "So this is where they came from?"

"Looks that way."

"Is there any way to tell from the surface where this comes out at?"

"I don't think so. It doesn't run at the same degree as your tunnel, so it could really come out anywhere in the mountains."

"So there's nothing I can do." I did not like the sadness in Cerridwen's voice. "This is too high up for me to block off, and there's nothing nearby for me to move my nest to. So all I can do is wait for them to come to eat my eggs, and hope that attacking them will be enough to frighten them off."

I was quiet as she spoke, and it just didn't seem fair to me. There wasn't any way for Cerridwen to logically spend her time constantly guarding her eggs. Foa had mentioned they could take a decade to hatch, and Cerridwen herself had said they wouldn't hatch for years. If she stayed here all the time, she'd be dead from starvation before that happened. There had to be another way.

The answer came to me, and I smiled. Granted, this was going to turn a lot of what I already knew about this world pretty much up on its head, but I didn't really care about that. All I cared about was making sure my friends were safe. All of them. "Or."

There was a long pause before Cerridwen responded. "I do not trust that 'or,' Mark. What do you propose we do?"

"You don't have to keep the eggs here, do you? All that matters is that your eggs, your nest, and yourself are safe, correct?"

"... yes?" There was confusion in Cerridwen's voice. "I'm afraid I don't follow you."

"The village is starting to raise centidragons as farm animals. I'm sure they'd be more than happy to help you build an appropriate nest in or near town as well, secure enough that no wild centidragons would come near and you'd have the additional protection of the town itself for your babies."

I could hear the shocked expression on Cerridwen's face when she spoke. "You want a dragon to live among humans? Freely? And you think that all the townspeople would be perfectly fine with this?"

"You would afford the village some protections in exchange, of course. Jun?" I couldn't see him in the darkness, but his input was needed. "It's your village. I'm the outsider here. But that seems to me, at least, to be the only logical option. What do you think?"

Jun was silent for a time before clearing his throat. "M'lady, we have a section near town where we have begun clearing land to expand the village in the future. I believe this would serve as a much better use of that land, and I'm positive the elders would agree. There are still a considerable number of trees left to clear out, but with your assistance we could remove them fairly quickly, then set about construction of a habitat suitable for you and your family."

"You... you would want me there? Even after I attacked the village?"

Jun's voice was quiet. "You attacked the village, but you attacked it because you thought we'd slaughtered your family. There will be much to discuss with the elders, and some of the townspeople will likely have some concerns, but they are good people. They will come to understand."

"They know you brought me to their village in the first place," I added. "You could have hurt me while I was asleep. Instead you showed me this world, helped me to learn and understand. You didn't have to do that, but you did."

"I... I don't... I mean... huh. Well then. Humans really can be quite a surprising bunch. Alright. For my family, I agree." There was the sound of some movement as Cerridwen walked over to her nest. Her voice was a bit more distant as she continued, "But the next problem. How do we get my eggs down to your village? I could carry them while I fly, but I can't carry them and walk at the same time."

Jun said, "I could lash them to your side if I had some rope, but all mine is at the village. If we can head back..."

"No!" It was almost a snarl. "I'm not going to leave my eggs unattended! What if the beasts return?"

I knew what I was going to have to do. I did not like it. Not one tiny little bit. This was going to be worse than cleaning the worst clogged Pipe I'd ever cleaned, even the one I'd worked on that had been so full of psychoactive drug residue that I had hallucinated for two full weeks.

"Jun, you don't have anything handy that I could use to start and keep a fire going, would you?"

"No, not that I can think of, why?"

I sighed. "Great. Well, here's what we're going to do then. Cerridwen, I need you to take Jun back to the village. You two need to tell the elders what is going to happen, then you need to get the rope and get back here quick. Then we'll tie these two eggs securely to Cerridwen's side, and get everyone to the village, safe and sound."

"Mark?" Jun's sounded concerned. "What, exactly, are you going to be doing?"

"Me? You said yourself that centis are skittish, and they won't come near if a human is around, right? Well, I'm going to sit right between those two eggs and wait for you two to get back. If I hear anything, I'll start making noise to scare off the centidragons."

"Sit here, in this absolute darkness, for hours? You'll go insane." Jun's voice showed his disbelief.

"You'd be surprised what a Worker can subject themselves to. Now you two go. And hurry! It'll still be a while before I get tired, but I do not want to fall asleep while I'm guarding the eggs."

"Oh, that would be bad."

"Mark." I felt Cerridwen move her head near to me, her warm breath washing over me as she spoke. "I don't know what to say. I almost..."

"It's alright, Cerridwen. It's alright." I reached my hand out awkwardly, making contact with scales after a moment. I had no idea what part of her face I was touching, but I patted it in a way I hoped was reassuringly. "What's done is done. No matter now. What matters now is getting you and your babies safe. So go. You and Jun get to the village and come back before I get tired."

"I will fly as fast as I dare, but I will not hurt your friend. We will return soon." Cerridwen cleared her throat, and flame reached toward the ceiling again. Once she pulled the flame back to her teeth, she knelt down to allow Jun access to her head and shoulders. When he was mounted, she let the flame extinguish and continued, "Stay safe, Mark."

"I will." I listened to them as her footsteps turned and quickly moved away. Soon enough, I was left alone with just my thoughts in the inky blackness of the world. My thoughts, and two eggs that were depending on me to keep them safe.

What was that curse Jun had used? Oh yes. By the three suns, what had I been thinking?

CHAPTER THIRTY-THREE – ABSOLUTE DARKNESS

I wish I could remember being a child. I know at some point, in my youth, I had sung songs. I remember singing, just not the tunes or the words. I just remember the act of singing itself. The Corporation knew that they could not start deprogramming us at too young of an age, and for a time, we were allowed to be human.

Singing would have been a great way to fill the empty void. I knew there was something in the void; after all, I was sitting inside the dragon's nest, surrounded by destroyed eggs and guarding the last two surviving ones against centidragons. But really, would they attack, knowing I was sitting right here?

I didn't know. I was still far too new to this world. None of this made much of any sense. "Especially," I said to no one in particular, "that I thought it'd be a great idea to sit alone in the dark for who knows how long guarding these eggs. Great idea."

There wasn't an answer, of course. I wondered how long I'd been sitting here. I hadn't gone to sleep yet, so it couldn't have been that long. That was one major comfort, if you could call it that. I knew I wasn't going to be trapped here. Once I fell asleep, I'd simply wake up in my world, though I would not relish the idea of returning here after that. No, Cerridwen wouldn't be very happy with me at that point.

I tried to think of how long they had been gone. I knew from previous flights that it took Cerridwen a little over two hours to reach the village from her cave entrance, and I really didn't know how long it took her to walk down the tunnel. Or how long it was going to take to gather up the stuff Jun needed.

A faint noise caught my attention, though I couldn't really turn and look in the direction of any noise. But then I heard it again. A faint scratching, perhaps? I listened intently, and sure enough, the scratching intensified. It was more than scratching, it was claws on stone and footsteps.

Something was coming. I had to make some noise, do something to scare away the centidragons. I reached down around my feet and picked up some of the discarded dragon egg shells. They were thick and heavier than I expected. These should do the trick quite nicely.

I started banging the broken shells against the ground, one after another, being mindful to keep the unbroken eggs behind me. The footsteps paused, for a moment, then continued on toward me, growing ever louder.

An amused growl rolled down through the darkness, and Cerridwen said, "It's us, Mark."

"Oh." I sheepishly dropped the egg shells and stood up. "You're back. Ah, sorry about that. Did you bring the rope?"

"We did." I heard Jun slide off Cerridwen's back and land rather awkwardly on the ground. "Ouch. Grabbed some fishing netting as well that should help keep the eggs a bit more secure. Go ahead and light up, Cerridwen, and Mark and I will get to work."

Cerridwen answered with a guttural bark that I had come to recognize as her fire lighting. It took me a few minutes to adjust to seeing again after so long in the total darkness of her nest, but once I could see we set to work. The unbroken eggs were heavy, and tying them to Cerridwen turned out to be difficult. Cerridwen was a big help with moving the eggs, as she was able to hold them in place while we secured them to her body with ropes and the netting.

Jun also had brought along something I really was hoping for. My stomach growled in appreciation as he handed over a few bread rolls and a water skin. It wasn't much, but it also wasn't food paste, and it was filling.

Soon enough, we were heading back up the tunnel for the final time, the eggs securely attached to Cerridwen's torso and Jun and I riding near her head. Cerridwen let the flame extinguish as we walked, though none of us had much to say.

Finally, Cerridwen said, "Jun, I must thank you again. For your village to allow me and my family..."

Jun interrupted her. "Think nothing of it, m'lady. We still have a lot of work to do ahead of us to set you up a proper home, so let's focus right now on just getting the little ones safe."

"Once we reach the entrance, I want to take them out of the netting." Cerridwen's voice held a mother's worry in it. "I would feel better carrying them in my claws than to have them strapped to me."

"I understand." I yawned, fatigue setting in. "We'll get 'em down for you..."

"Mark?" Cerridwen sounded concerned. "Don't fall asleep yet. This is not where you want to sleep. Not by any means."

"Oh, I know." I rather doubted I would want to return to the middle of a soon-to-be-abandoned dragon tunnel, in mountains I had no idea how to descend. Nor did I want to fall asleep in mid-air. I wasn't even sure how that would work. Would I just reappear the next day and fall to my death? I didn't really want to think too hard on that.

Jun said, "We should be at the entrance soon, Mark. Once we're in the air you'll do better, I'd be shocked if you could sleep during flight. Then when we land, we'll get you into a hut right away so you can go ahead and rest, alright?"

"That... that's fine." Jun was right, I was getting really tired. But I couldn't sleep. Not now. So I had to fight sleep, something no Worker ever did.

That was the longest time period of my life. Every few minutes, Jun would tap me on the back to ensure that I hadn't fallen asleep. More than a few times, I had drifted, so I was thankful that he watched over me. I at least learned that I didn't vanish immediately upon falling asleep, so that was something.

Finally, we reached the entrance of the cave, and I sighed with relief. One of the suns had already gone down, and the next was well on its way. It was getting cool with the lack of sunlight, so Jun and I worked quickly to bring the eggs off of Cerridwen's side.

Then, with both eggs gripped lovingly in her claws, and Jun and I holding on tight, Cerridwen took flight from her cave for the last time.

Jun had been right about one thing. It was impossible to fall asleep in the air. Not only due to the fact that we had to hang on or we'd fall to our deaths, but with the setting suns and the speeds we were moving, it was quite chilly. Staying awake wasn't a problem at all.

Soon enough, the village came into view, and Cerridwen aimed for a clearing where many villagers were already waiting. She approached and slowed down carefully. Her landing was awkward, since only two of her four feet were in play, but land she did. Once on the ground, she placed her eggs down carefully then moved so Jun and I could hop to the ground as well.

Foa approached with two other elders and nodded at the three of us. "Welcome back." He glanced at me. "Now, I assume someone is going to explain what, exactly, all this is about?"

I yawned. "Well, you're going to have to either have Jun or Cerridwen tell you, or you'll have to wait until I return tomorrow. But I'm about to pass out standing here, and we all know what happens when I sleep." I smirked. "I'm sorry, Foa, but it's been a long day, and I'm really tired."

Foa nodded, a smile crossing his face. "That's completely understandable." He looked up at the dragon. "So, Cerridwen, is it?" At her nod, he gestured with his walking stick. "I'm assuming that you will be perfectly alright out here tonight?"

Cerridwen met Foa's gaze evenly. "Do you know of any predators stupid enough to come between a mother dragon and her eggs when she is nearby?"

"Fair point."

I felt a hand on my arm, and I looked over at Iri. She smiled and motioned for me to follow, which I did so willingly. She led me away from the hustle and bustle of the villagers and dragon toward a small building near the centidragon pens.

As we entered, I yawned again. Fatigue was settling in, hard. "I'm exhausted."

"I bet. Jun told me to set you up someplace close, so I grabbed this hut for you." She motioned to a blanket and a thatch pillow set on the floor nearby, next to a window. A small meal was ready for me, and the smell was divine. "And you shouldn't wake up with the building on fire this time around." Her eyes twinkled. "Eat up, it's fresh."

"No, I'd hope not. Once was enough." I nodded thanks to her and gratefully moved over to the food. A quick bite told me that it tasted better than it smelled, and I started wolfing it down greedily. "Thank you, Iri."

"You're welcome, Mark." Iri moved to the door and paused before she closed it. "Good night."

CHAPTER THIRTY-FOUR – REBELLION

I watched Allen limp his way to the bus stop and shook my head. For all his bravado yesterday, I had a feeling he was more hurt by the Enforcer than he let on. I understood why he needed to show the Workers what he did; we needed to see that they weren't going to kill us, that we could make a stand without fearing for our lives.

Looking at him now, though, I'd be hard pressed to say it was worth it. But there were a lot of Workers. Having sheer numbers on our side would help matters. I nodded as he approached. "Allen."

"Mark." He winced as he came to a stop at his spot. "The day after a beating is always worse."

"This a normal thing for you?"

"This isn't the first time I've been beaten by an Enforcer, no." Allen sighed. "Not even my fifth time, I'm sad to say."

"Really?" I raised an eyebrow. Maybe I'd underestimated him again. Standing up to those things once was insane. Multiple times? "Huh. Guess you really do think we deserve better."

"Of course I do. Which is why today's the day." Allen glanced at me, noticing the blank expression on my face. "You haven't forgotten that, have you?"

I blinked. With all that had happened yesterday, I had indeed forgotten. "Um."

"Heh. It's alright. I pretty much expected you to have forgotten, what with your other world and all. Have a lot going on there last night or something?"

"You could say that."

"Anything you can talk about?" Allen looked around. "No one's here yet, and probably won't be for a few minutes."

"You wouldn't believe me, but sure." I sighed. "Basically, I spent the day flying to a dragon cave. Once inside the cave, I guarded her eggs in pitch black darkness so that centidragons wouldn't eat them while she flew back to the village to get rope and some netting. When she returned, Jun and I tied the eggs to her, and we flew back to the village, and I went to sleep. That was my day."

Allen looked rather lost. "Uh... ok." He shook his head.

"You asked."

"Yes, yes I did. And I'm not sorry I asked, but one day you'll have to explain to me what a dragon is."

"Soon as I figure out how to explain it, I'll tell you."

"Deal."

We lapsed into silence as the other Workers started to arrive. When the bus pulled into its stop, something odd happened. The doors opened, but instead of the Workers on board getting off, we immediately filed on, filling up the rest of the space in the bus.

There were no empty seats, so we were forced to stand. Two of the previous rotation Workers stood up, however, to allow Allen to sit down, as it was obvious he would not be able to stay upright the entire trip down to the work site.

It struck me then. This was really going to happen, wasn't it? There wasn't any turning back from... well, whatever it was we were going to do. I really wasn't all that clear on what Allen had planned. I'm sure he had done some planning with the other Workers, but that had been during the night when I wasn't around.

They could have held their meetings in my home for all I'd known. So no matter. I'd see what they had planned soon enough.

The ride was uncomfortable but not overly so, and soon enough the bus pulled to a stop at the work location. The previous cycle was waiting to get on the bus, but when they saw us, they turned as one and joined us.

Immediately, the Boss started screaming. He was nearly incoherent, but I could make out some of what he was screaming into a nearby communication port. He yelled the words, "Revolt, mutiny, help" and a few other words I didn't quite understand over and over.

Allen immediately started directing us. He stood as tall as he could and shouted, "Workers! Head to your work benches and grab any tools you can! Grab your blowtorches! Grab your wrenches! Give them a reason to pause if they try to attack you!"

So we did. Some of us grabbed wrenches, hammers, magnetic sledge hammers, all manner of tools normally used in the construction and maintenance of the Pipes. I took my trusty wrench and tucked it into my belt, grabbed my fusion blowtorch and a few foam expanders in case something caught fire near me, and after a nod in Allen's direction, took off running toward the heavy ionizers.

I had driven the heavy machines a few times before, so their controls were familiar to me. A dozen Workers followed me over to the ionizers, each going to another machine. Allen must have organized that as well. I nodded to myself. The man certainly was thorough.

I climbed into the seat of the nearest ionizer and pushed the start button, letting the beast hum to life under my touch. It was a good sized machine, about the size of the bus I'd ridden down into the Pipes. It would definitely help if things went sour, but hopefully...

"Workers!" Allen's voice interrupted my thoughts. He had climbed up to where the Boss had been standing. The Boss had vanished, and Allen was now speaking through the same communication port that the Boss had used. It was loud enough that all the assembled Workers could hear him. "The time has come! It is time to regain your humanity, prove your worth, take what is rightfully yours!"

The assembled Workers roared in unison. I did not. Something was bothering me. Where did the Boss go? As Allen continued speaking, I scanned the crowd. But everywhere I looked, it was nothing but Workers.

Workers to the left, carrying tools and cheering for Allen. Workers to my right, either climbing on or driving the ionizers, looking less and less like Workers and more and more human by the minute. I had to give Allen credit, at least he'd inspired us to start thinking for ourselves. That had to count for something. By the bus, Workers listening to Allen, nodding and agreeing with whatever he was saying, their tools in their hands or on their belts.

And behind Allen, far down the road and just arriving past the bend, the first Enforcer turned the corner and streamed at us at top speed. Then another, then another.

I stared in shock as my mind registered what I was seeing. A full two dozen Enforcers were heading straight for us, and everyone was too busy listening to Allen to notice.

Of course, I was in a heavy ionizer. It wasn't like I was helpless. Ignoring Allen at this point, I rotated a few dials and set the nose of the ionizer so that it pointed a few meters ahead of the approaching Enforcers. I waited a moment, then mashed the activation button with my thumb.

The result was noisy and instantaneous. My ionizer made a high-pitched wail and a beam of light shot out, impacting with the road in front of the Enforcers. The road expanded outward and exploded, leaving a gaping hole twenty feet wide and fifteen feet deep.

Two of the Enforcers were close enough to the explosion radius that they were thrown to the side. Debris from the road shattered their armor and knocked them flat. They did not get back up. The other Enforcers ignored the loss of their comrades and went around the new hole and continued toward us.

The Workers noticed the Enforcers now. Allen had as well. "Workers! Mark has the right idea! Do not let them get the upper hand! Charge and meet them with your tools before they attack! Charge!"

As the Workers roared, emboldened by my attack and Allen's words, I couldn't help but wonder if maybe, just maybe, this wasn't the best of ideas. But it was too late. Two of the Enforcers lay on the ground, either dead or out of commission; I wasn't sure which, since I wasn't entirely convinced that they were even alive. The Workers were running at the Enforcers, all manner of tools coming to bear against their opponents.

This was going to get messy.

CHAPTER THIRTY-FIVE – UNINTENDED CONSEQUENCES

It took less than thirty seconds before everything became complete and utter chaos. Once the first Workers reached the Enforcers, the remaining twenty-two Enforcers acted in unison and lashed out as a single entity, mercilessly striking the entire front row of Workers with their electrical monofilament whip arms.

Seven Workers dropped almost immediately, writhing in pain as electricity arced through their bodies. One Worker with electrical protection in his boots managed to catch the monofilament whip, grabbed his magnetic riveter from his belt and proceeded to rivet the whip onto the road. In a moment, the Enforcer was effectively immobilized held by his arm to the road.

But that was a short-lived victory. The Workers were not warriors, and the Enforcers had no mercy. The first wave of Workers were soon decimated, with only the initial two Enforcers and the immobilized Enforcer as the losses on their side.

"Mark!" Allen's voice was desperate, and I did not have to look his way to know what he wanted. If the Enforcers got much closer, they'd wade through the remaining Workers with ease and shut down this work stoppage for good.

I looked at the other Workers on the ionizers and shouted, "Well, what are you waiting for? Use those things!" Following my own advice, I mashed the activation button without bothering to see where it was aimed.

My ionizer ate a hole in nearly the exact same spot that it had done so the first time. This second shot was farther back, and did nothing

175

else helpful since the Enforcers had already moved past the crater location.

I shook my head and spun the dials to move the impact zone as I heard the other ionizers around me spin up. As they began to fire, I smiled. We were not totally helpless. We were not going to die. This wasn't a total abject failure. I was going to go back to the village again!

Every single ionizer shot was completely off the mark. The Enforcers waded into the bulk of the Workers by Allen without mercy, and the smell of sizzling flesh rose up into the air. As Allen had said, they weren't trying to kill us, no... but they certainly weren't going easy on us either, and no Worker was used to physical punishment in any fashion.

The screams of agony from the wounded were brutal. However, our sheer numbers worked to our advantage, for they simply could not hit every Worker at once. At first, only one Worker slipped past an Enforcer's defenses to land a hit or two. But once one managed to do so, another did. Then another.

Then one did so with something more effective than their wrench. A hit landed from a sledge hammer. A follow up with the fusion blowtorch. And suddenly, the tide was turning.

Those of us on the ionizers watched as twenty-two Enforcers went to twenty, then to fourteen, then to six, then to just a single one remaining. A cheer filled the work zone when the final Enforcer slipped to the side and fell over with a thud, sparks shooting from mortal wounds.

I heard Allen saying something, probably something inspirational, but I was too preoccupied counting. By my guess, almost all of the first group of Workers to meet the Enforcers had been taken out of commission. Of the second group, we'd lost about half. We still had my cycle of Workers, of which a third of us were manning ionizers, but that didn't leave many of us still on our feet.

Granted, there were still plenty of cycles of Workers that were due to arrive throughout the day. Once they did, they'd bulk out our numbers. Every Worker was behind this little rebellion of Allen's, so it was only a matter of time before we swelled to full strength. Each bus that arrived would bring more and more.

I heard a cry from one of the other Workers in the ionizers, and I turned in his direction. He pointed back down the road where the Enforcers had first arrived, pale with terror. I didn't want to turn and look. Maybe if I never looked, whatever it was would never materialize.

I had to look.

I immediately regretted turning around. Coming down the road were another fifty Enforcers. These were led by five wheeled objects I did not recognize. The objects were square, with a sort of shimmering effect to the air around them, and four wheels guiding them as they rolled along. Otherwise they were completely nondescript and non-threatening.

Fifty Enforcers. The Corporation had no intention of talking, or of listening. This was to silence us, and immediately. If those fifty reached us, it'd all be over.

I glanced at the other ionizer drivers, and we came to an unspoken agreement. Those Enforcers could not reach Allen and the others. It was up to us. As one, we spun the dials on our machines and aimed.

I could hear Allen shouting something, but it was impossible to hear him over the noise of the ionizer. I aimed directly at the front line of the Enforcers; to heck with slowing them down, it was time to stop them and stop them permanently. My decision made, I activated my ionizer.

My beam reached out its lethal rays along with its brethren, fired by my companions. All were aimed as I had aimed, directly at the Enforcers.

And all impacted a shimmering field that sprang up from between the devices that were in front of the Enforcers. The field redirected the beams away, where they slammed into the walls with concussive force.

That must have been what Allen had been trying to warn us about. Those were shield generators leading the Enforcers. Our ionizers were now useless. They had prepared for everything.

Anger welled up inside me. It wasn't fair. It just wasn't fair. Furious, I depressed the activation button and held it down. Beside me, I heard additional shots being fired by the Workers in the other ionizers; we all had the same idea. Overload the shields with superior firepower. My ionizer fired once, then again, then again, then again. Over and over and over, our shots ricocheting off the shield uselessly as the Enforcers drew ever closer.

The shots went everywhere, reflected randomly by the moving shield. An ionizer shot was unique; they did not disperse over time. They had to be spent with an impact with solid matter before they stopped. Ionizer shots went to the ceiling, to the walls, to the support beams, behind us, around us, and into the lava below.

"Mark!" I finally heard my name over the din of the ionizer. I looked at Allen, and the look of sheer terror on his face as he waved both arms at us in a desperate attempt to get our attention caught me by surprise. I released the button, letting the machine stop firing as I tried to hear what he was telling us.

That's when I heard it: the deep, low rumbling of earth moving. I thought the sensations and vibrations I was feeling were coming from the ionizer activating underneath me; I was wrong, dead wrong. As the Enforcers had continued to move forward as we fired, our shots had ricocheted in every direction.

Some of those shots had gone in some very unfortunate directions. The impacts against ceiling, support structure and walls had taken their ultimate toll, and cracks were now spreading across every surface. Faster and faster they raced as the structural integrity of the massive cavern degraded, threatening complete collapse at any minute.

There was nothing anyone could do. As one, the Workers simply watched as the ceiling collapsed. It started small. Just a few stones where moving cracks forced them out. But then larger stones fell, and still larger ones, until boulders emerged and descended into the pools of lava below.

Then it all came in a rush. With a massive crack and a roar of finality, the ceiling snapped nearly in half and everything above us moved almost two hundred feet straight down. We had no chance.

My last thought as the first boulder crashed toward me was, oddly enough, of Iri. I wondered how I'd tell her I wasn't coming back, and how I'd ask her to take care of the centidragons. Then there was an impact, a lot of pain, heat, and darkness.

CHAPTER THIRTY-SIX – COMING HOME

It was raining again. I felt the heavy drops trying to invade my sleep, forcing their way past my slumber without fail. Try as I might to ignore the sounds and continue sleeping, the rain was insistent. Finally, I gave up and woke.

That's when the pain made its presence known. There were parts of my body that hurt that I wasn't aware I had hurt. I didn't understand though... why would I hurt...?

Oh. The memories came back in a rush, and my eyes popped open, though I immediately shut them again. The light was far too bright. But that didn't make any sense, the light was always heavily moderated...

Wait. Bright light. Rain. I opened my eyes again, carefully this time, and breathed a sigh of relief when I realized I was in the other world. I looked up into the sky, and saw a most wondrous sight.

The sky was partially cloudy, and what clouds were there were dumping out a decent amount of rain, which is what had woken me. However, the clouds were also somewhat dispersed, allowing enough blue sky to allow at least one of the three suns to shine down unaccented by the clouds. It was... I couldn't remember the word. I had only heard it a time or two in my life, and only in this world.

Ah. I remembered the word. Beautiful. The word was beautiful. I stared at the sky for a while, watching the rain and the clouds until I decided I need to try moving.

That turned out to be a mistake. The minute I tried to stand up, pain shot down both legs and it felt like I had completely crushed my feet. I grimaced and looked down at my legs, regretting doing so. My legs were covered in dried blood and were obviously broken. My feet were, for lack of better term, completely pulverized.

I suddenly had a vision of large boulders crushing the ionizer I was driving, and me with it. I remembered Enforcers, and Workers dying, and Allen, and...

"By the three suns." I paled, looking at the damage to my legs and feet. "What have we done? They... they're all dead, aren't they?"

There was no answer. I needed no answer. I had answers in my severely mangled legs and feet. There was not going to be any walking for me anytime soon.

But where was I? I grimaced and looked around. I was in a field, a large one, and a fair distance away the forest started with some large trees. Off farther in the distance were the mountains, surrounding my field of vision with peaks as far as I could see.

This was odd. This was the first time I hadn't reappeared in whatever spot I'd fallen asleep in. So where had I ended up? I tried to prop myself up on one arm to get a better look around, but I slipped and fell back.

Grimacing, I tried again and made it up to one arm. There was something familiar about this place, but what? As the rain continued to fall, I finally realized where I'd seen this location. I'd been here before, the first time I'd come here. This was the clearing I'd shown up in the very first day. If I were able to walk, I'd find a tree that was missing a chunk of bark about the size of my thumb from its trunk.

And I bet it still tasted terrible.

So why was I here?

After not getting a satisfactory answer in a few minutes, I frowned. This wasn't getting me anywhere. I needed to get to some form of shelter if nothing else. I was thankful for the rain; if it had been a clear day, the three suns would have been quite hot, and I wasn't sure how I was going to get to the trees and their shade.

Better to find out now, I suppose. I sighed and tried one more time to stand, but the pain in my legs and feet told me that wasn't about to happen. Standing and walking weren't happening.

No, this was going to have to happen the hard way. I started trying to pull myself toward the trees, one pull of my arms at a time. It was incredibly slow going, and incredibly tiring.

It was during this effort that I made another discovery. As I crawled, something kept poking me in my sides. I investigated the source and found that I had managed to bring my wrench and fusion blowtorch with me from my world.

This didn't surprise me after a few moments of thought. I had brought a splinter from this world into my home world, after all; I'd just never had anything on me from my world to bring here. So when I'd been knocked unconscious and had my wrench and fusion blowtorch in my belt, they'd naturally made the transition with me.

Tools could come in handy, I mused, provided I survived to actually make use of them. My fusion blowtorch wouldn't help me much; it had been crushed along with my legs, so I discarded it. My trusted wrench, however, was just fine. It would take more than a boulder to crush that metal.

After a time, the rain stopped and the clouds parted. As I expected, with the three suns out to play, the day became warm in a hurry, and my wounds began to hurt in ways I'd never experienced before. My forward progress was slow, agonizingly slow; I had no real point of focus to tell whether I was moving forward or just crawling in circles.

Finally, the pain was too much and I passed out. When I came to, the suns had moved quite a bit across the sky, but little else had changed. With no other real option presented to me, I grit my teeth and began crawling again.

I made it farther that time before I again succumbed to the pain and fell unconscious. When I woke up the next time, I was on my back, staring into a view that I was having problems processing. The sheer beauty of it was beyond my comprehension, and it was enough to make me forget the pain as I stared in rapt wonder.

The three suns had all set. The sky was black as tar, yet it was alight with millions of tiny pinpoints of light. These lights flickered and twinkled merrily far, far off in the distance. Some were slightly bigger than the others, for what reason I could not fathom.

Against the backdrop of this soup of pinpointed light was a thin spider web of dim, distant white fire, draped almost lazily across a full third of the night sky. It appeared to be a misting of light, the way it was diffused against the darkness of the night sky.

As I watched, an occasional streak of flame would dash from one edge of the world above me to the other. A trail of fire would follow the point of light, chasing the pinpoint into oblivion.

The fantastic beauty of the daytime sky could never compare to this. Even Joe hadn't mentioned ever seeing a sky like this before. Clouds floating lazily across the heavens was one thing, but whatever this was that I was watching was something else entirely. I'd have to ask Jun or Iri...

It hit me at that moment. They didn't know where I was. I didn't know where I was. No one knew where I was. I was in the middle of nowhere, badly wounded, and I didn't know if I was going to vanish when I managed to sleep on my own accord. No one knew I was even here in their world or how to find me, and the odds were pretty darn high that I was dying.

Lucky me.

CHAPTER THIRTY-SEVEN – THE DOT IN THE SKY

Two days passed. I wasn't able to accurately judge how much progress I made toward the trees; I had given up trying to prop myself up to see, because that took too much energy I needed for crawling. I was getting slower and slower, and was spending more time just simply staring up at the sky, waiting to die.

That hadn't happened yet, of course. I had run out of options and ideas. At that point, I just wanted to crawl until I couldn't crawl any further, so at least I could say that I never gave up.

I would at least give myself that. But even that was falling by the wayside as I was now wracked with fever from infection. The wounds in my legs had worsened, and without treatment, well... they weren't going to get better anytime soon. They would stop hurting eventually though. About the time everything stopped hurting.

Granted, at this point, everything hurt including my skin. I'd discovered that my skin had started turning a reddish coloration from the exposure to the three suns. Every movement made even the skin on my ears hurt, which I hadn't realized was even possible before now.

The one consolation I found in all this was that, after two full days, I hadn't yet returned to my home world. Something had changed, and I was apparently here for good.

Not that this benefited me much at this point. I sighed and watched as first one, then the second of the three suns appeared over the horizon. It'd still be a little while before the third sun appeared, and I'd learned this was the time frame for my best opportunity to get some crawling in before it got too warm. It gave me the best light for viewing without too much heat.

But today, I just was too tired. Maybe it was the fever, but I just wanted to sit and watch the three suns come up. Maybe today was the day that I'd move on to whatever awaited in the beyond. That's all I wanted. To let the pain stop, to sleep, and just put all this nonsense behind me. But until then, I'd watch the skies.

There wasn't a cloud in the sky to interrupt my fevered musings. Not a single, solitary cloud, but there was some sort of strange black dot. That was unusual. I looked again, sure I was seeing things. But sure enough, there it was. A dot, clear as day, obstructing my lovely view of the sky. I reached my hand out to it, trying to wipe it away; but whatever it was, it wasn't directly in front of me. It was considerably farther away than what I could reach with just my hand.

Disappointed, I reached into my belt and pulled out my wrench. Darn it all I was going to fix that speck in the same way I fixed a Pipe! As a bonus, when I held the wrench up to fix the speck, it covered up one of the two suns, affording me a bit of shade so I could see what I was doing. But after a few minutes of holding my wrench up to the speck, it occurred to me that I didn't really have any idea how, exactly, I was supposed to use the wrench on it. It didn't have a nut I could turn. I couldn't just whack it and fix it that way. It simply wouldn't reach.

Irritated, I left the wrench in the air while I contemplated this issue; but after a few minutes, the wrench grew heavy in my hand. I let it land beside me with a thud, and I sighed.

My gaze went back up to the skies, and I frowned. Was the spot bigger? It was! The spot was bigger, almost twice the size it'd been when I had first noticed it! Spots weren't supposed to get bigger. I realized it was probably my fever getting the best of me, so I turned away and looked toward where the third sun was just starting to peek over the horizon.

Once the third sun had awoken and started his climb up into the sky, I finally chanced another look toward where the spot had been. It was still there, and was even larger still. How in the world?

Wait. I peered up at the spot, trying to concentrate through my fever. Something about the spot seemed strangely familiar. But I couldn't place my finger on it. As I stared at the speck, the world started to close in on me, and I recognized the signs that I was passing out again. I tried to fight the approaching darkness, but the tunnel vision closed in. I tried in vain to focus solely on the spot.

When I regained consciousness, it was considerably later in the day. The three suns had moved in their travels across the sky, and a light cloud cover had moved in to offer some shade. To my disappointment, the spot in the sky had disappeared.

So much for feverish entertainment. It felt like it had ebbed for a few minutes, so without anything else to do, I figured I'd start crawling again. As I began to painfully move again, I heard it. A low thrush of wind, a rumble of wings, something I'd heard a time or two in my journeys in this world.

I recognized it in an instant. Dragon flight.

I tried to prop myself up on an arm, to try to get a glimpse where the sound came from, but my strength failed me. I need not have bothered, however, as soon enough the sound was overhead, and Cerridwen was directly above, looking down at me. She was high enough that though I could tell that two people were riding on her back, I could not make out who they were.

She landed somewhere behind me, and I heard footsteps as she approached. Not long after, smaller and faster footsteps joined hers, and I heard human voices shouting my name.

Within a minute, Jun and another of his hunters that I did not recognize were by my side, their eyes wide as they saw me clearly. I tried to talk, but my voice was not forthcoming; too many days without water had stolen it from me.

After they had recovered from the shock of seeing my wounds, the two men went to work. They unrolled some form of large fabric-based tarp and carefully moved me onto it. This sent pain shooting back through my legs, but it could not be helped. Next, they placed some long rods through some holes in the fabric and used rope to secure it. Then, they crisscrossed the rope over me until I was strapped in.

I felt my fever rising again as Cerridwen walked over and peered down at me. "You're going to be alright, Mark. We're going to take you home."

I couldn't respond.

Jun and the other hunter said something I couldn't hear to Cerridwen and clambered up onto her neck. Next thing I knew, we were up and away, the clearing I'd found myself in disappearing behind us.

I had no time to enjoy the flight, however. Not long after we climbed into the sky, the tunnel vision returned and I slipped back into unconsciousness, this time with the sensation of floating making for one very odd feeling.

I hoped this feeling wasn't dying, but something told me I'd be alright.

CHAPTER THIRTY-EIGHT – RECOVERY

When I woke next, my first thought was that I was lying on something soft. My next was that I felt absolutely no pain. No pain whatsoever. This was immediately followed by the realization that I felt nothing at all. Pain, touch, hot, cold, nothing but the weight of the blankets on me. I frowned and tried to sit up.

When my body flat out ignored me, I sighed. It was going to be one of those days, apparently. I heard movement beside me and a familiar voice say, "Oh, good, you are awake, my boy. How are you feeling?"

I tried to turn toward the voice, but only managed to move a few inches. I wanted to answer, but the only thing that came out of my mouth was a dry croak.

"Oh! Oh dear, my apologies. A moment." I heard some movement before Foa moved into view with a small cup. "Here, try to drink this. It's going to likely be messy, but that can't be helped right now."

He held the cup up to my mouth carefully, and I tried my best to drink. As he'd promised, it was quite messy. My mouth felt numb, and it was difficult to swallow, but I managed to get some water down. Once I was able to drink, my voice returned. "Ugh. Thank... thank you."

"You are welcome." Foa set the cup down and smiled. "It's quite good to see you awake and moving, Mark. You gave us quite a scare, you know."

"Trust me, that was not by choice."

"I would not say so, no. We were rather worried when you did not reappear that morning. Cerridwen was beside herself with worry and spent most every day looking for you when she wasn't guarding her eggs. It was she that found you, you know."

"I... yes, I think I remember that." The memory of dragon flight, and of being lifted into the air came bubbling back up from somewhere in the recesses of my mind. "How did she find me?"

"Ah. Very curious, that." Foa reached under the bed and grabbed an object off the floor. "During one of Cerridwen's searches, she saw something reflecting light from the ground. When she went to take a closer look, she found you. She saw very quickly how bad of shape you were in and realized she wouldn't be able to carry you back with your injuries, so she returned to the village to get help."

"Reflecting?" I thought for a moment, trying to remember. "What was reflecting?"

"This." Foa held up my wrench. "Curious object, I must say. Is this from your world?"

"Y... yes. That's my wrench." Amazing. As much as it served me at home, it saved my life here. I gazed at the simple piece of metal with a new respect. "I had it on me from my home for once when I came here. So she came back to get help?"

"Yes. She was greatly worried she'd hurt you if she tried to carry you back in the state you were in. She figured, and rightly so, that we'd have a way to get you back safely. Jun and Yoq, a hunter I'll have to introduce you to one day, set up a stretcher for you that they strapped to Cerridwen."

Foa adjusted his position slightly and motioned at my legs. "You are probably wondering why your body feels numb."

"A bit, yes."

"You can thank the elders, Alo and Leu. We might be a small out of the way village, but Alo is probably one of the strongest bone healers this side of the continent. Between her medicines and cantrips, and Leu's superb skills at blocking pain, they should have you back on your feet in a few weeks."

"That's... that's insane. My legs were... Oh no." I paled as the memories of how they'd gotten that way came rushing back. "Oh no. No, no. They're dead."

"Who's dead?" Foa raised an eyebrow and looked at me with kind eyes. "Relax, Mark, getting upset isn't going to help you right now."

"Everyone. The Workers at home, they're all..."

"Mark." Foa placed his hand on my chest, stopping me. "Calm down." He waited for me to stop talking before he continued. "You've been through a lot. That much is obvious from the condition of your body. Everyone in the village, including myself, is very curious as to how this all came to be. But no one wants you to tell your story before you're ready to do so, and the important thing right now is healing, not moving around. Too much of that will make your healing take longer than it has to, and no one wants that."

He moved his hand and smiled gently. "Now, if you feel up for telling me, I won't stop you. But if you do so, please do so slowly, and calmly."

"R... right." I swallowed, and I told Foa everything. How the Workers had stopped working, how the Enforcers had come, how it looked like we had stood a chance until the second wave of Enforcers arrived, how the Workers on the ionizers kept firing until the roof collapsed, and waking up in this world. I told him how it'd been a few days now. How I hadn't returned home again, how I wasn't sure why I didn't appear where I'd gone to sleep, and that I was positive everyone else back home was dead.

Through it all, Foa listened. He would occasionally help me get another drink of water when my words dried out my throat to the point that talking hurt, but otherwise he simply let me speak. He asked for clarification on things he did not recognize, such as the Enforcers. Otherwise, he simply let me talk at my own pace, letting me spill and heal as he knew I needed to do.

Once I was done, he was quiet for a few minutes. "Well. If there's any positives to be taken from that, Mark, it's that your friends died standing up for themselves." Foa stood and walked over to a window. "It might be small consolation, but from what you've told us of your world, it might be the bravest deaths they could have hoped for. They died trying to change the world. That is not a needless cause to die for."

"But they still are dead." My tone was flat.

"Yes, but they were alive before they died, yes?" He glanced at me out of the corner of his eye. "From what you've told me, most of your time there you were barely living. You were simply existing, little more than tools. Worthless. You even thought yourself as such, correct? But not at the end.

"No. At the end, when it finally mattered, they thought of themselves as important. They died as men, not as tools. They at least had that chance."

"Allen gave them that chance." I sighed, feeling miserable now that the weight of what we had done finally landed on my shoulders. "And we failed him. He was trying to warn us, and we kept firing. We brought the ceiling down. We killed ourselves, didn't we?"

"Perhaps. Perhaps not. I wasn't there, so I can't say." Foa turned away from the window and walked back to me. He sat down and placed his hand on my shoulder. "However, if the ceiling hadn't collapsed, what would have happened?"

I blinked. "What?"

"Think carefully. You said your, what did you call them? Ionizers? They had become ineffective against the Enforcers, correct? So you had a large group of Enforcers approaching, a good portion of your Workers were already wounded, and your weaponry was unable to work. What options did you have? What would have happened if they had reached you?"

"Um..." I thought for a moment. "Well... if they had reached us, we would have all gone to reprogramming for a long time. We would have had our memories chemically wiped until we barely even remembered our names, and eventually we'd have been right back into the Pipes, working like nothing had happened."

Foa's eyes met mine. "Then you would have died without being dead. Their lives would have been meaningless. This way... they meant something."

He was right. I felt a moistness at my eyes, an odd feeling in my gut that I couldn't understand at the realization he was right. Their lives were gone, but they hadn't been meaningless. They had been worth something, and in the end, they had stood for something.

We had all stood for something. We had stood against the Corporation, for once in our lives. It had cost us our lives, true, but by those three suns burning outside, we stood against them. We had stood as one, fought as one, died as one.

I blinked away the moisture in my eyes and smiled half-heartedly at Foa. "In a way, it doesn't seem fair."

"What doesn't, my friend?"

"That I was able to make it out, and no one else was. Why I, of all the Workers in the Corporation, was the only one chosen for this."

"How do you know that?" Foa raised an eyebrow again. "This is a big world, Mark, and from the sounds of it yours was too. Didn't you tell me about another in your world that spoke of things he couldn't possibly have seen?"

Then it hit me. Joe. Could he have really...?

Foa read the answer from my face and smiled. "You see? You might not be the only one. For all you know, you might not have been the only Worker visiting different worlds. Who knows?" He patted my arm and stood up. "Not I. But for now, you must rest. You need time for the medicines and cantrips to start restoring your bones, and sleep would be best for that."

"I..." I sighed. I still couldn't come up with the right words for everything I wanted to say. "I just... tell everyone that I said thank you, Foa."

"You can tell them yourself in the next few days. Most everyone will come through here to see how you're doing." Foa's eyes sparkled. "Especially Iri. She's been worried sick about you since you didn't wake up where she left you."

"She has?" I hadn't thought about that. I was going to have to apologize. It really wasn't my fault, was it? I mean... I looked up as Foa started to laugh. "What?"

"Nothing, my boy, nothing. I'll explain it to you later. In the meantime, go ahead and get some sleep. You'll need it."

He nodded farewell to me and closed the door behind him, completely ignoring my total confusion. As sleep came, unbidden, I still wondered.

What was he talking about?

CHAPTER THIRTY-NINE – MY OWN TWO FEET

The next few weeks passed by rapidly. I learned who Alo and Leu were immediately. Both of them came into what I learned was now my permanent home on a routine basis to renew their medicines and cantrips, as well as to see how I was healing. They applied their medicines, did their alchemy thing, asked me questions, made me do various and often painful exercises that increased in intensity as I healed, and left around lunchtime.

Alo was a very small woman with sharp features that honestly frightened me a little. I could smell her coming before she ever entered the home; it was a sharp, though not unpleasant, scent that reminded me quite heavily of pools of lava. Her fingernails were long and curved, and each time she touched me I was certain she drew blood. Yet every time she pulled her hands away, there was never a wound, nor a trace of blood. She was the village elder that worked with bone, and her cantrips hurt when she administered them. After she was done, however, I could physically see a difference in my legs. It was amazing to watch.

Leu was a very friendly, beast of a man that reminded me of Jun. He also had a very distinct scent, though nothing as strong as Alo's; his was an earthy scent of growing plants. I found out later he was actually a cousin of Iri and Jun, which explained the resemblance. When he spoke, the whole house shook with his voice; but his hands were gentle when he administered his medicines, and the potions he gave me took all the pain away.

Between the two of them, I watched my legs heal faster than I would have thought physically possible. Bones that were shattered pulled themselves together over the course of days and regenerated over the span of a week that should have simply never healed again. Sinew reappeared and reattached itself to new bones underneath the skin as though it had been there the entire time. It was simply incredible.

It was through watching my wounds heal that I realized again just how different this world truly was from my own. This world might have three suns. It might have centidragons. It might even have a dragon sitting outside waiting on me to heal enough to come out and pay my regards to her... But, it took watching myself heal from wounds that should have crippled me to make me realize just how truly different it was. Nothing could compare to that.

I still was hesitant to try walking, which Alo assured me was a smart decision. I'd need more time for the bones and tendons to fully heal before I walked on them. Mindful of their warnings, I was content to stay in my new home and rest. To keep me company, Iri brought me food a few times a day and would spend hours with me, talking and teaching me about her world. Sometimes she was accompanied by Jun if he wasn't out hunting, and together they filled me in on the day to day dealings of the village.

One morning when I was particularly down from having to stay inside, Iri and Jun surprised me by bringing two centidragon hatchlings to visit. Alo was quite unhappy to have the two hatchlings running around my home and, in her words, "destroying her cantrips," but Leu laughed and got down on the floor with Iri and Jun to play with the hatchlings. They spent the better part of the day just letting the creatures roam about, and even Alo had to admit that the mood had brightened considerably.

To my delight, it didn't take long before I no longer needed Foa's potion to stomach the village food, and I quickly developed favorites among the dishes. A particular fruit, a star-shaped thing that I still

couldn't pronounce the name of quite right, was far and away my favorite. Iri usually giggled when I asked for it, since most of the adults
in the village tended to regard it as a fruit that only children ate; adults
usually found it too sweet.

A side effect of some of the various cantrips I received was that I
started to dream clearly for the first time in a very long time, and with
the dreams came memories. I started to remember my family. Though
it was still hard to picture them clearly, I realized the two figures in my
dreams had been my parents, and the other children had been my sib-
lings. And I... I felt fairly certain that Allen and I had had more in common than I'd realized, because the more I remembered, the more positive I became that I'd been given to the Corporation as payment for my
parents' debt.

I asked Foa about this, and he was unable to give me an answer,
since he was not familiar with the world I came from beyond what I'd
told him. But he said that perhaps, over time, more memories would return. For the moment, I was to focus on my rehabilitation, and let my
mind heal when it was ready.

Finally, after a time, I was able to start walking, albeit slowly. Iri was
with me, of course, as I took my first hesitant steps out of my house to
look around what was now my village to call home. I gaped in amazement at how much the village had changed since I had last seen it. It
had been three months since I had been discovered in the clearing, and
they had made considerable progress in building both Cerridwen's new
home and the centidragon pens.

For Cerridwen, a large hollow stone mound had been erected for
the dragon's nest. No entry or exit could be found at ground level,
giving her privacy from the humans when she desired it for her and
her eggs. It towered nearly thirty feet tall and was an impressive sight.
When I asked Iri where the stones had come from, I discovered that
Cerridwen had brought the stones from the mountains, two at a time,
for weeks on end.

Against the backdrop of the dragon nest were the centidragon pens and centidragon runs. Where before they had only a single pen, the village now had a full dozen pens and the runs spanned an area nearly as large as the village itself. The wood and stonework of the pens had been coated in the paint I had suggested, a very bitter tasting paint to keep the centidragons from eating it.

Iri introduced me to the new centidragons, whom were very eager to meet their new handler. I learned that Cerridwen was clearing the mountains of the wild centidragons, one by one, and bringing the eggs she found back to be raised by the village. Any adult centidragons she killed but didn't eat she brought back for the village to use for cantrip materials. Iri told me that the tamed centidragons wanted nothing at all to do with the dragon and were terrified to go anywhere near her, which suited Cerridwen just fine.

During my rehabilitation, Iri was with me every step of the way. I found myself looking forward to her arrival and regretting her departure more and more. I didn't understand these thoughts and feelings at all.

When I brought these strange feelings up to Foa, he smiled cryptically and mentioned that I should address them with Iri directly.

So, I did.

One night before she left for the evening, I asked Iri about the strange feelings I had been having about her. I told her that though they weren't bad feelings, but I didn't understand them, and was quite confused. I hoped she could help me gain some clarity regarding them. So many things about this world I didn't understand, but these feelings especially were new and different.

She just smiled at me and said she understood. She moved to the candles and blew most of them out, one by one. She left a few of them lit, however, and then sat beside me on the bed. She took my hand in hers, looked deep into my eyes, and smiled ever so shyly.

It took a few minutes and then I, too, began to understand.

CHAPTER FORTY – CHANGING THE WORLD

Throughout my recovery, one person I never found time to talk to was Cerridwen. The dragon was keeping herself incredibly busy; between continuously updating the construction on her new home, hunting for wild centidragons in the mountains, and helping out with forest removal for the village, it was all I could do just to find out where she was located at any given moment.

I had a feeling I knew why, but I wouldn't know for certain until I asked her. And that was proving more difficult than fixing a Pipe with your bare hands. But finally, one sunny afternoon, Iri and I managed to find her clearing out the forest with a few of the villagers. As we approached the forest's edge, we watched one tree fall after another in rapid succession.

I still wasn't moving all that fast, but I had only a slight limp by this point. Iri and I walked as fast as I could toward the sounds of industry, and soon enough Cerridwen and six of the villagers came into view.

I stood in awe for a moment as I watched Cerridwen work on the trees. Cerridwen had told me before that humans feared dragons, and given her size, claws, teeth, and fire breath, I'd pretty much figured out the reasons why. Watching her cleave through a full-sized tree with a single swipe, then grab the tree and carefully maneuver the entire log onto the ground with little effort showed me just how much strength truly lay within the frame of a dragon.

It struck me how easily she could have slaughtered the entire village if she'd taken the mind to. Thankfully, she'd relented that first day and waited for me on the second. I shook my head to clear my thoughts as Iri and I made my way over to the working group.

The villagers were the first to notice us, and they greeted us heartily. Cerridwen waved hello with the tree in her claw, a very impressive sight. We picked our steps carefully through tree debris as the group continued to work.

It was quite a thing to watch. Cerridwen would take the felled trees in her claw and remove most of the larger branches with a swipe or three of her back foot. She would then lay the tree trunk down on the ground and the villagers would get to work with axes, removing the remainder of the smaller branches.

Soon enough, the tree was ready, and Cerridwen would pick the now-stripped log up and place it with the others that were ready to go, all in a line. These logs would be gathered later and, pulled via ropes back to the village to be used for hut construction, fence building, and other purposes. The tree debris was collected and piled up, where it would be used for smaller construction purposes and in the villagers' fires. Nothing went to waste.

Iri squeezed my hand. "You go talk to Cerridwen, Mark. I'm going to go talk to Zac, he needs to stop feeding Lannor all those extra branches. That ornery centidragon's getting the taste for wood, and is starting to try to eat his way out of his fence. I think he's even starting to like Foa's horrid paint."

"Give 'em hell." I returned her smile and watched her walk away before I spun on my heel and made my way over to Cerridwen.

Cerridwen made herself comfortable as I approached. "Good afternoon, Mark. It's good to see you up and moving about. The last time I saw you, I wasn't sure you were going to survive the night."

"And I have you to thank for a good portion of that, if my memory is right." I carefully sat down on a tree stump nearby. "You carried me back to the village, didn't you?"

"That was me, yes." Cerridwen nodded. "After I saw how badly you were hurt, there was no way I could carry you without hurting you further. I didn't know of anything else to do, so I came back to your village, and two of the humans said they had a way to carry you safely. They returned with me and did just that.

"Which, I might add, that device they used was quite an ingenious little idea on their part. I'd never realized humans were as inventive as they're turning out to be. I have much to learn about your kind."

"Thank you for coming for me, Cerridwen. I'd be dead if it weren't for you."

"How could I not come for you?" The dragon snorted. "You are my friend. I will admit I was worried sick when you had not appeared as you normally did in the morning. Then when a female human came to me and asked me to look for you, I had no reason to say no. She was rather insistent that I search."

I chuckled. "That would be Iri, I'm assuming."

"The lady you arrived with just now?" At my nod, Cerridwen continued, "Then yes, that is her. She seems to be a very happy, very strong female of your species. Is she your mate?"

"I believe she has chosen me, yes." I smiled.

"Treat her well. She is a good person."

"I will. Do you remember how you ended up finding me? You said you saw me from the sky." I looked up into the clear sky, shielding my eyes as best as I could from the glare of the three suns. "How in the world could you have seen my small form from as high up as you were? My memories from the time are pretty muddled, but I think I remember seeing you in the air, and you were extremely high up."

"That's the odd part." Cerridwen thought for a moment. "I was heading to the mountains. I wasn't even planning on stopping in that section of forest until something caught my eye. It was a flash of light. Once, then again, over and over. I'd never seen the like, so I had to go see what it was. When I got close, the light became unimportant as I saw you and how badly hurt you were."

Cerridwen's voice grew quiet. "I've thought about that flash of light a lot since that day, during your recovery. I don't know how or where it came from, but..."

"Cerridwen." I smiled. "Was it something like this?" I pulled my wrench out of my belt and angled it so it was between her and three suns. Then, I just had to move the wrench a bit.

"Ahh!" Cerridwen closed her eyes as the bright light of the suns reflected across her face. "Yes! That was it! So that was you?"

"It was." I shook my head. "In my fevered state, I saw a dot in the sky. I wanted to fix the dot, so I took out my wrench and tried to fix it. By doing that, I accidentally signaled you."

"What is that object?" Cerridwen inspected it as I held it up for her. "Such a small thing to create such a strong light. How does it work?"

"It's my wrench, from my world. It doesn't make light, but it's made of bright metal, so it reflects light really well. Since there are three suns here, there's plenty of light to reflect. Other than that, it's nothing special."

"It's from your world, so that makes it special." Satisfied, Cerridwen changed the subject. "So you know, Mark, when my eggs hatch, I have every intention of raising my family in direct contact with you and the other humans of the village."

"Oh?" I raised an eyebrow in surprise. "That's unusual, isn't it?"

"It is indeed. But meeting you, then working with the villagers has taught me much about humans. Enough to realize that I know far too little about your kind, and I would like my children to grow treating your people as equals.

"Foa and the elders have said that my family and I are welcome here for as long as we wish. Though I doubt he realizes how long of a time frame that could potentially be, I'm going to take him up on it. My kin would call me insane, but I have to do what I know in my heart is right."

I shook my head. "Someone I once knew told me, you can't be sane if you want to try changing the world."

"Sounds like he was a wise man." Cerridwen stood and stretched her wings.

"He was."

EPILOGUE

I t still amazes me how fast time moves now that I'm out of the Pipes. Before I knew it, it was four years later.

So much changed, so very fast. At her request, Iri and I moved into the same house together. When our son was born, Iri said there was only one name we could possibly give him. I weakly protested, wanting to stick with the village tradition, but I really should have known better. I will never win an argument against Iri when she's set her mind to it. So now little Allen serves as a reminder to me daily of where I'm from, where I've been, and how much further I still have to go.

I will not fail you this time, Allen. I promise you that.

As I stood there, watching Iri head out into the grasses to bring in the last two centidragons, I was struck again by just how odd this was. I could still remember turning my wrench in those damnable Pipes.

I was reminded of just how far I'd come. When I woke up that morning, the day Joe jumped under that bus, how could I have expected anything like this? Of dragons, of villagers, or of finding a family? A shadow passed overhead, and I gazed upward with a smile and a wave. A roar of greeting met me as Cerridwen flew past.

She'd mentioned to me the week prior that her eggs had hatched recently. Once they were able to fly, she wanted them to come out and meet the villagers and especially me. Cerridwen wanted her family to start the process of getting dragons and humanity to work together.

I couldn't agree more. I looked up as a rumble of feet indicated another centidragon was incoming. I shook my head as first one, then another centidragon charged into the pens, eager for their meal. "Never fails, does it?"

"It does not." Iri walked up to me on the other side of the fence and looked up into the sky. "Cerridwen flying over spooked them, though, and when they saw me coming their way, they immediately thought food. So here we are."

She glanced back toward the village. "Have you given any more thought to what Foa asked last week?"

"About going to the bigger cities to see if anyone there has had experiences with other dreamwalkers?" I shook my head. "I have not, not yet. I'm not quite ready to go looking for answers to questions I don't even know how to ask."

"You'll have to eventually, Mark." Iri's tone was gentle. "Even if just to see the big cities of our world for yourself."

"I know. I'll think about it." I pulled the gates to the centidragon pens shut for another night. "So, where to now?"

Iri vaulted over the fence with practiced ease and laced her fingers in mine. "Well, we'd probably better go rescue Jun. He's had Allen all day. He's either spoiled the poor boy rotten, or he's wishing he'd gone hunting instead of getting stuck babysitting."

"Sounds like a plan."